Putuguq & Kublu

INHABIT
MEDIA

Iqaluit • Toronto

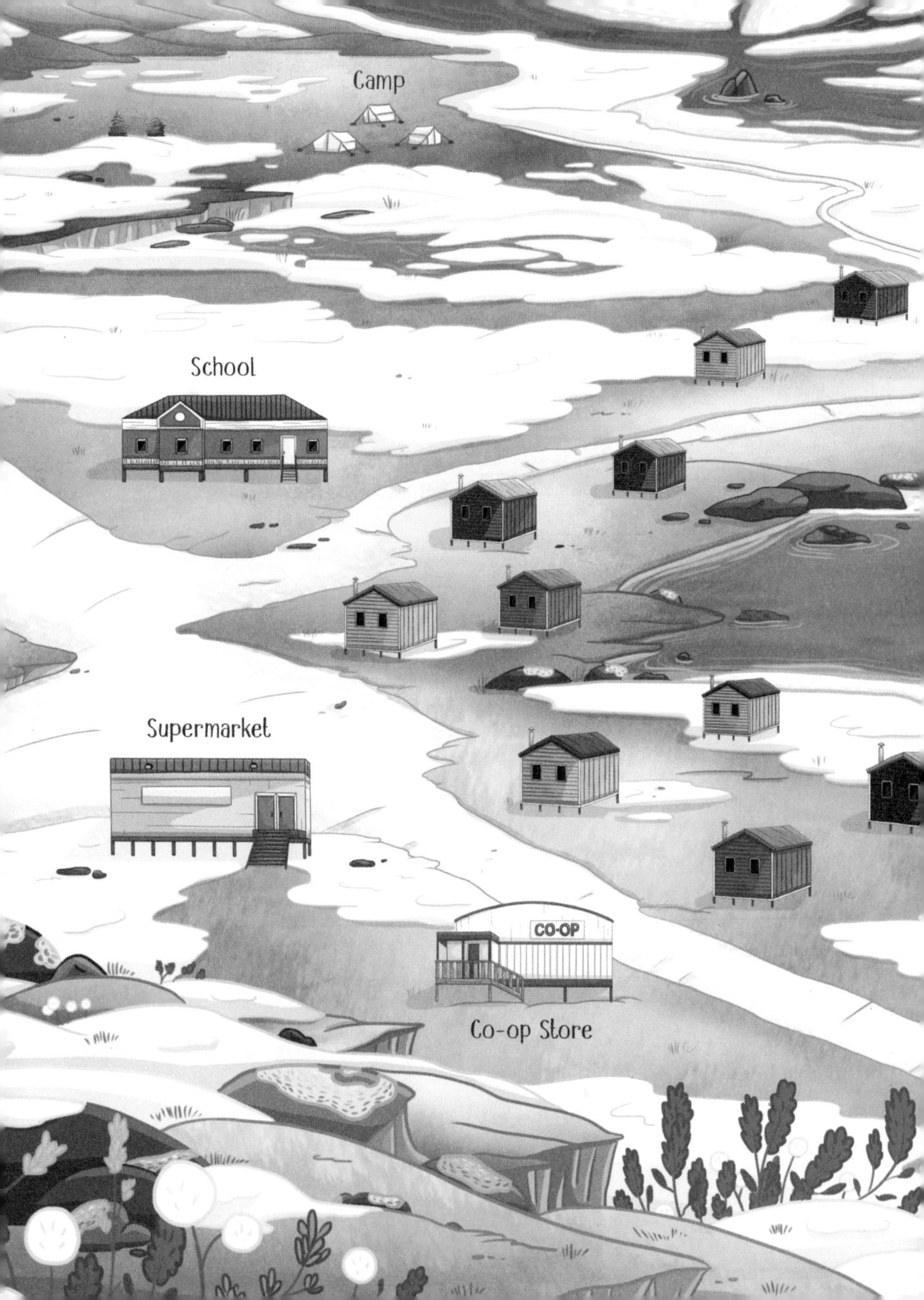
Camp
School
Supermarket
CO-OP
Co-op Store

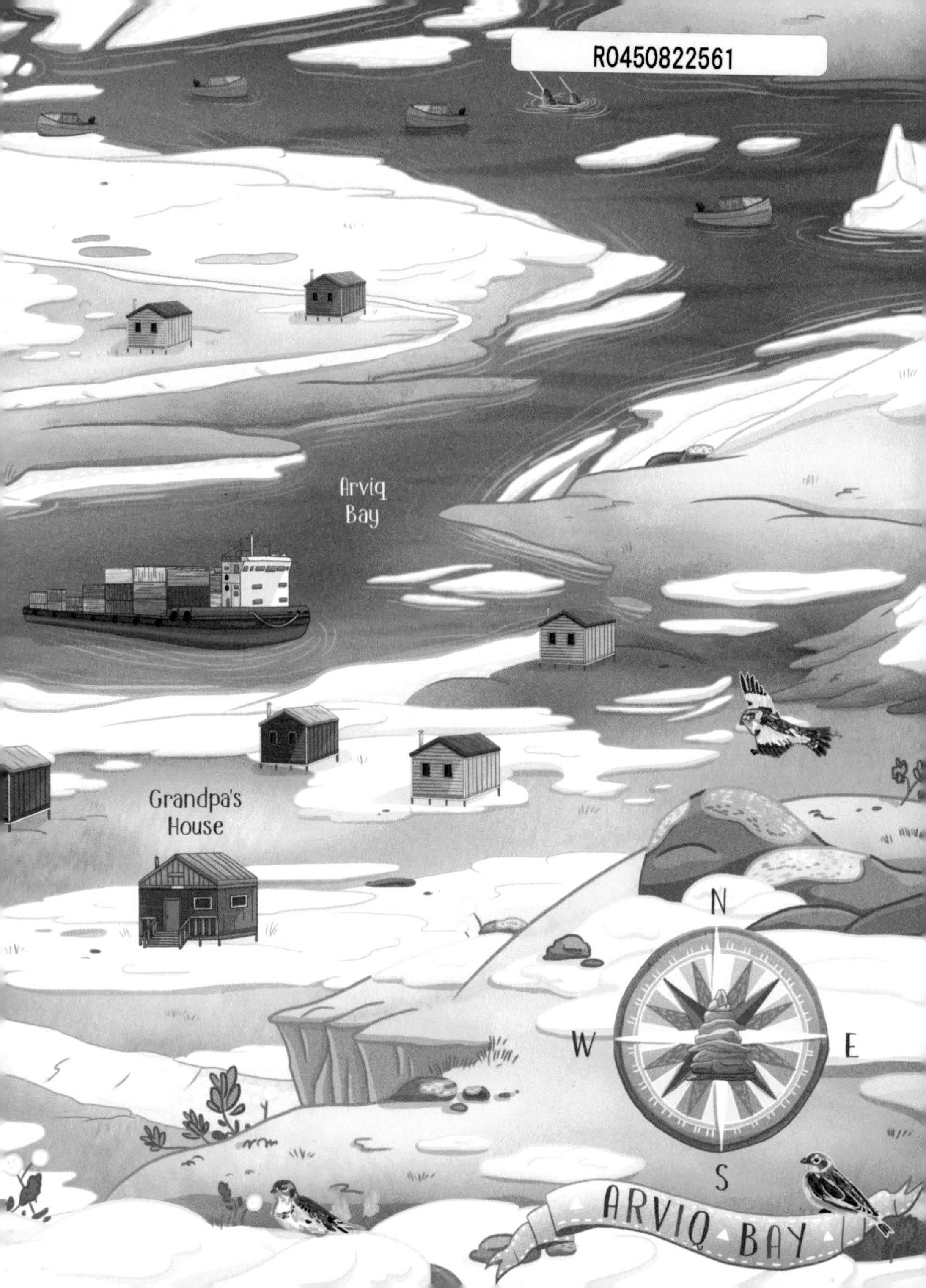
Arviq Bay
Grandpa's House
N
W
E
S
ARVIQ BAY

Published by Inhabit Media Inc. | www.inhabitmedia.com

Inhabit Media Inc. (Iqaluit), P.O. Box 11125, Iqaluit, Nunavut, XOA 1HO
(Toronto), 191 Eglinton Ave. East, Suite 301, Toronto, Ontario, M4P 1K1

Editors: Neil Christopher, Louise Flaherty, and Danielle Webster
Art director: Danny Christopher
Designer: Astrid Arijanto

We acknowledge the support of the Canada Council for the Arts for our publishing program.

This project was made possible in part by the Government of Canada.

ISBN: 978-1-77227-143-0

Printed in Canada.

Library and Archives Canada Cataloguing in Publication

Christopher, Danny, author
Putuguq & Kublu / Danny Christopher ; illustrated by Astrid Arijanto.

ISBN 978-1-77227-143-0 (softcover)

1. Brothers and sisters--Comic books, strips, etc. 2. Brothers and sisters--Juvenile fiction. 3. Inuit--Comic books, strips, etc. 4. Inuit--Juvenile fiction. 5. Comics (Graphic works) I. Arijanto, Astrid, illustrator II. Title. III. Title: Putuguq and Kublu.

PN6733.C5365P88 2017 j741.5'971 C2017-901931-7

Canada

Canada Council for the Arts
Conseil des Arts du Canada

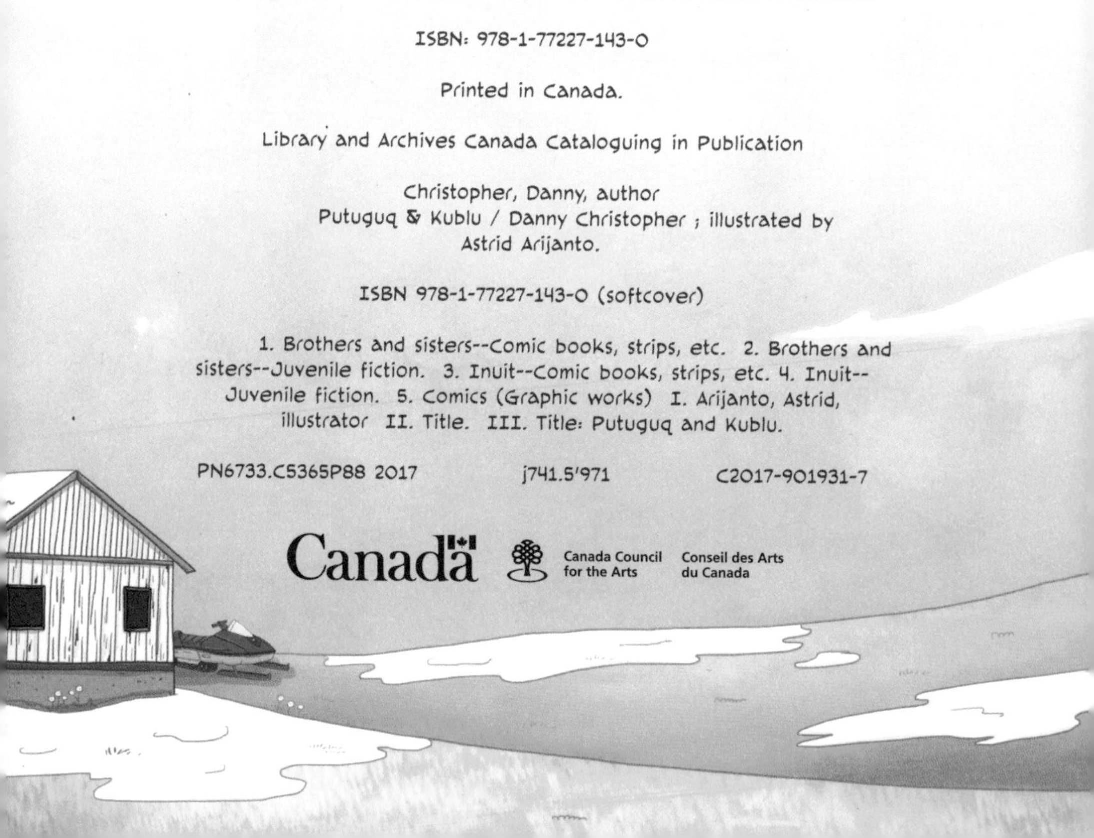

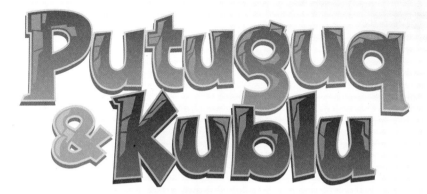

Putuguq & Kublu

By Danny Christopher
Illustrated by Astrid Arijanto

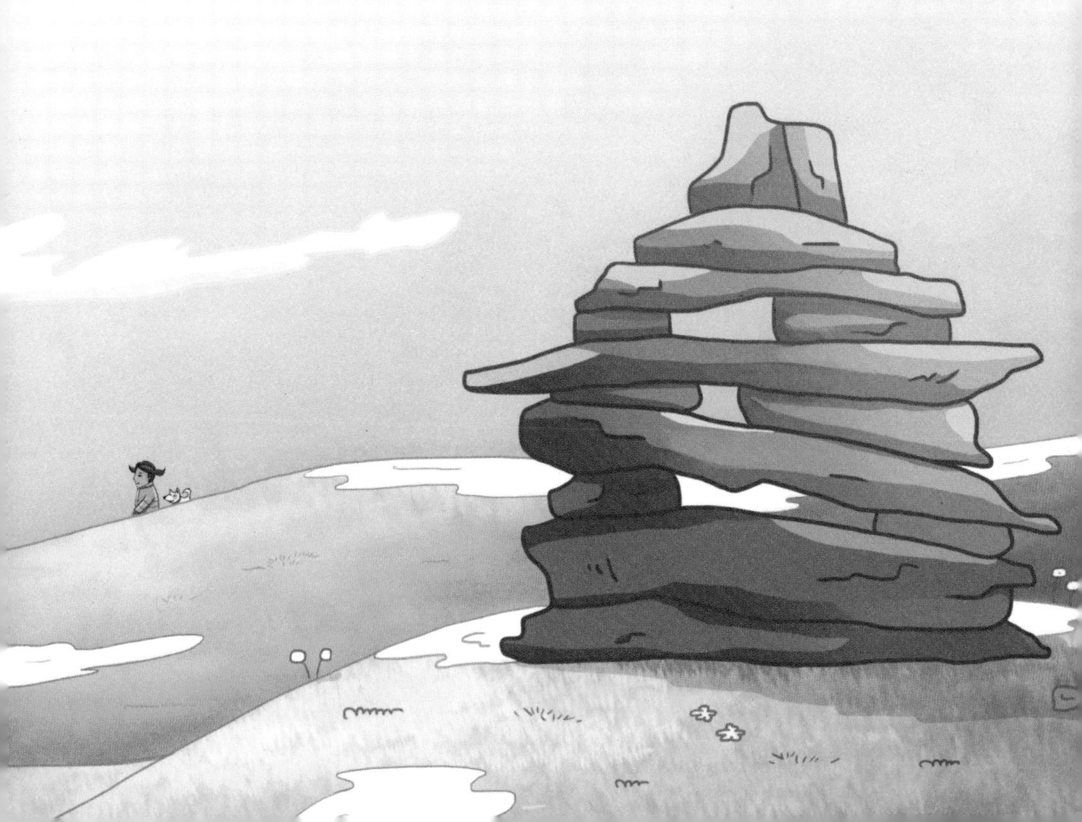

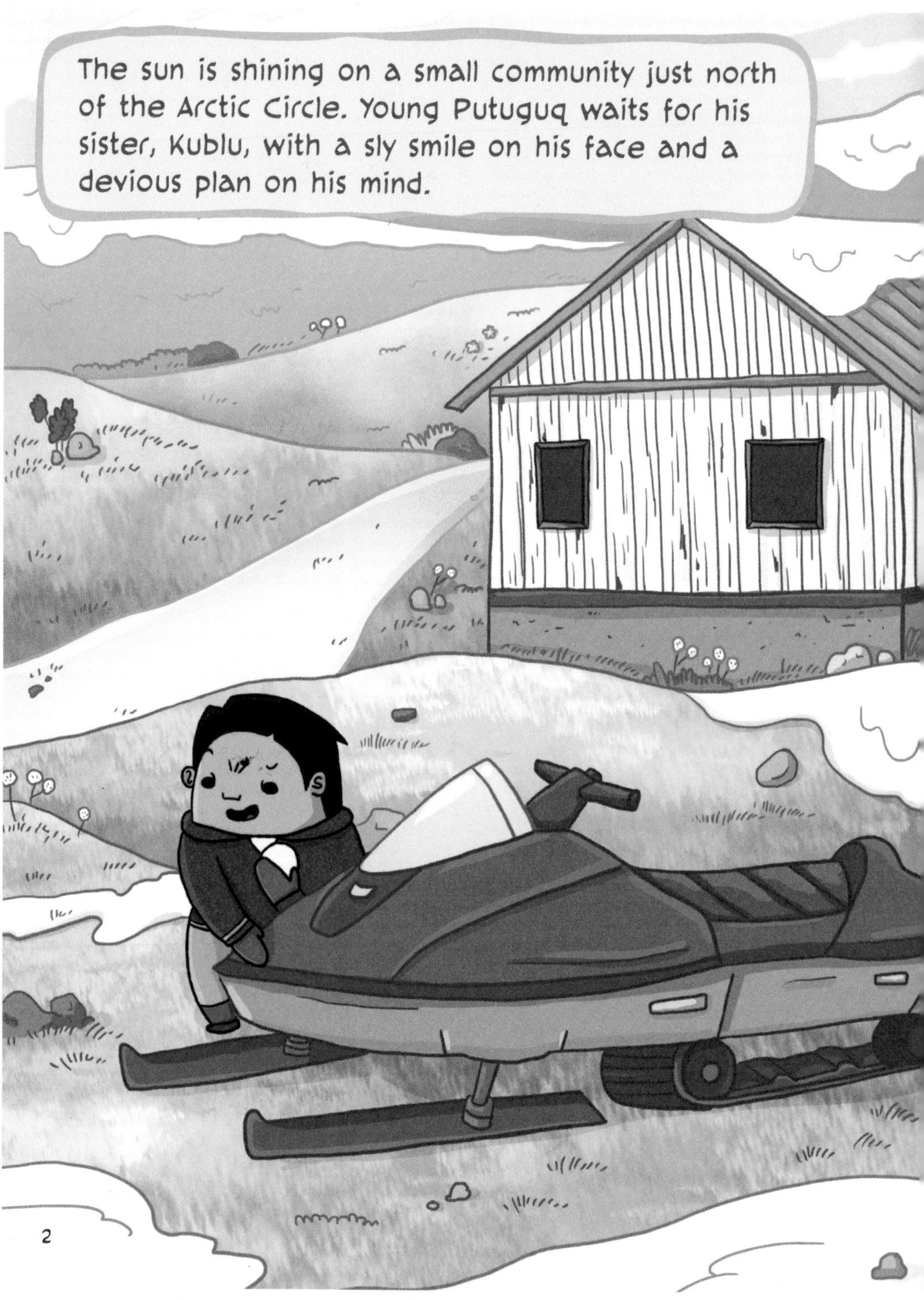
The sun is shining on a small community just north of the Arctic Circle. Young Putuguq waits for his sister, Kublu, with a sly smile on his face and a devious plan on his mind.

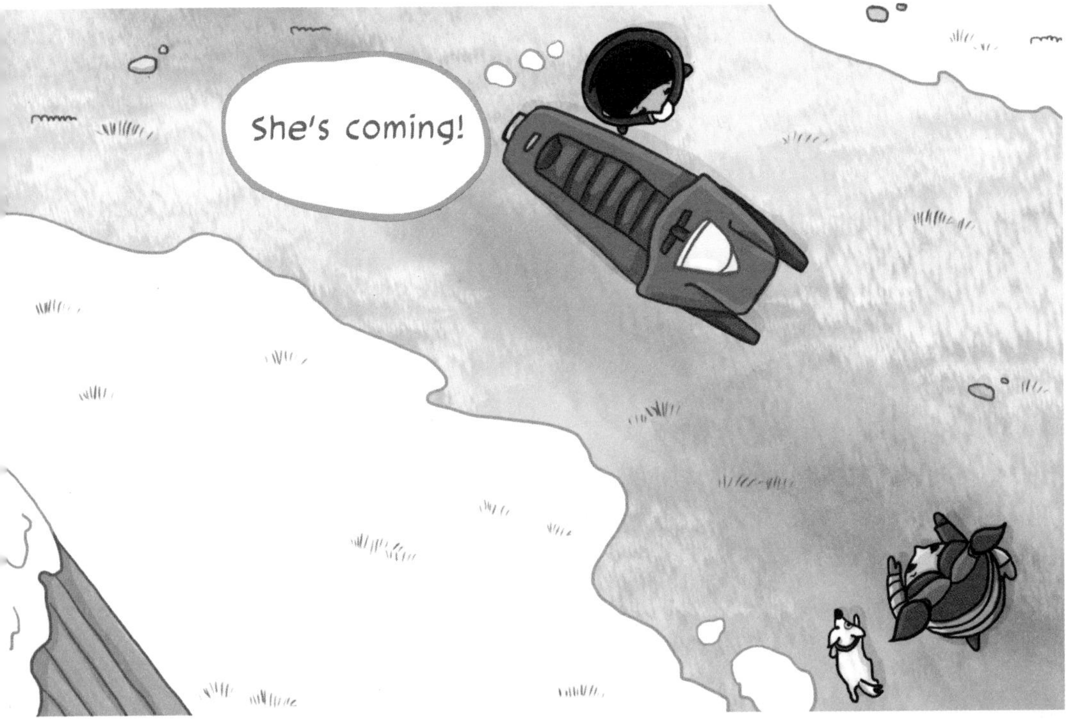
She's coming!

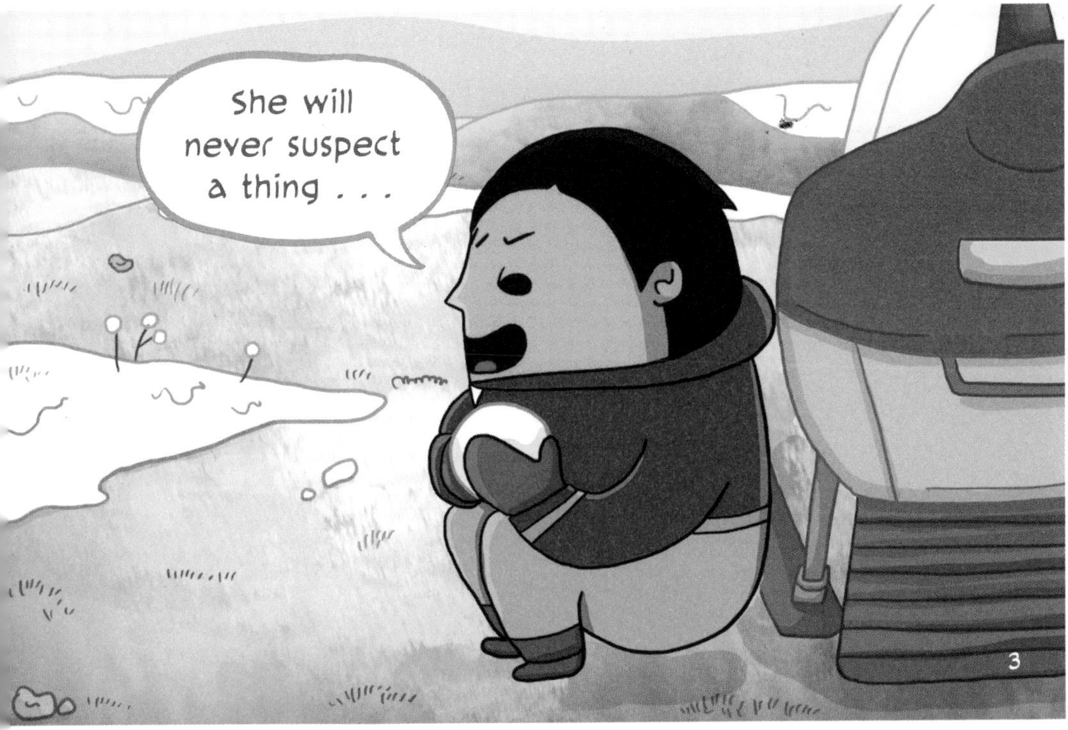
She will never suspect a thing . . .

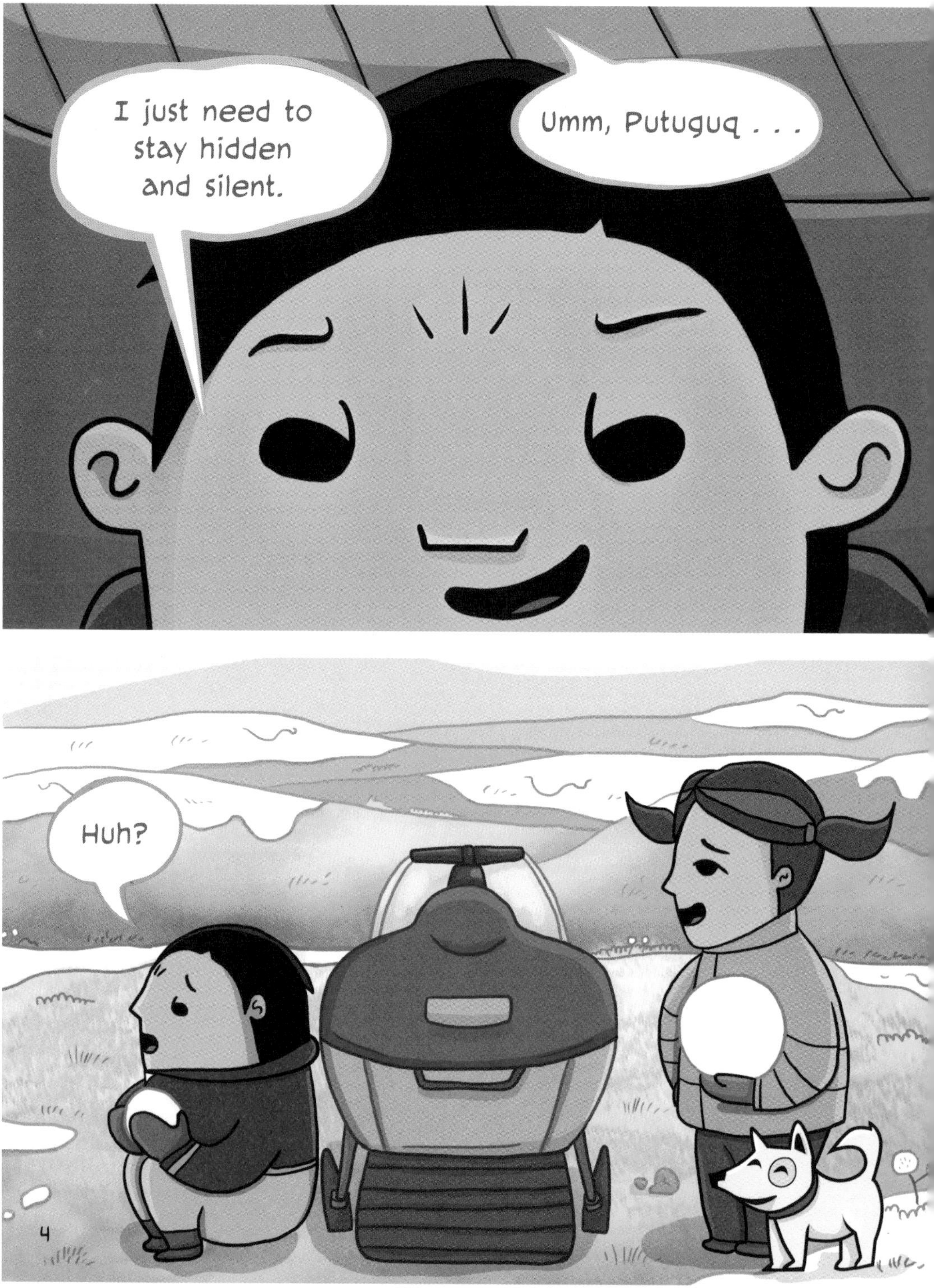
I just need to stay hidden and silent.
Umm, Putuguq . . .
Huh?

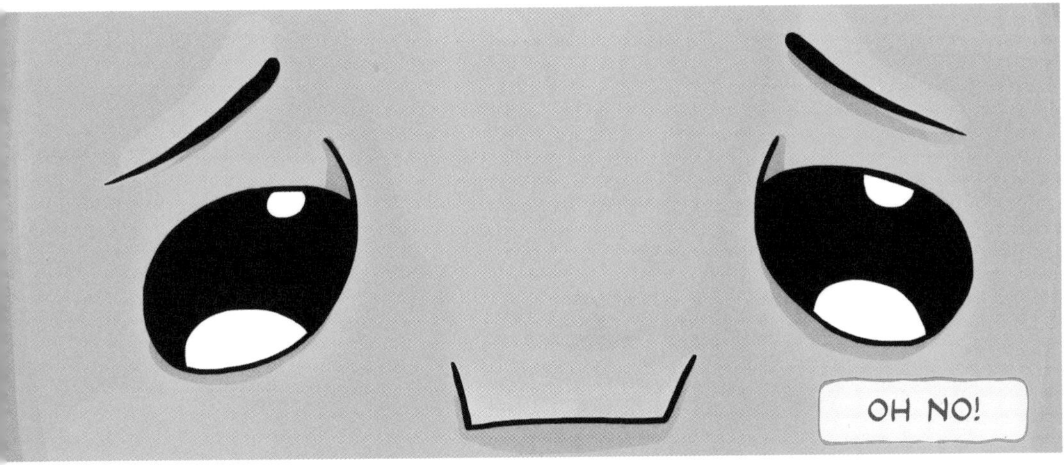
OH NO!

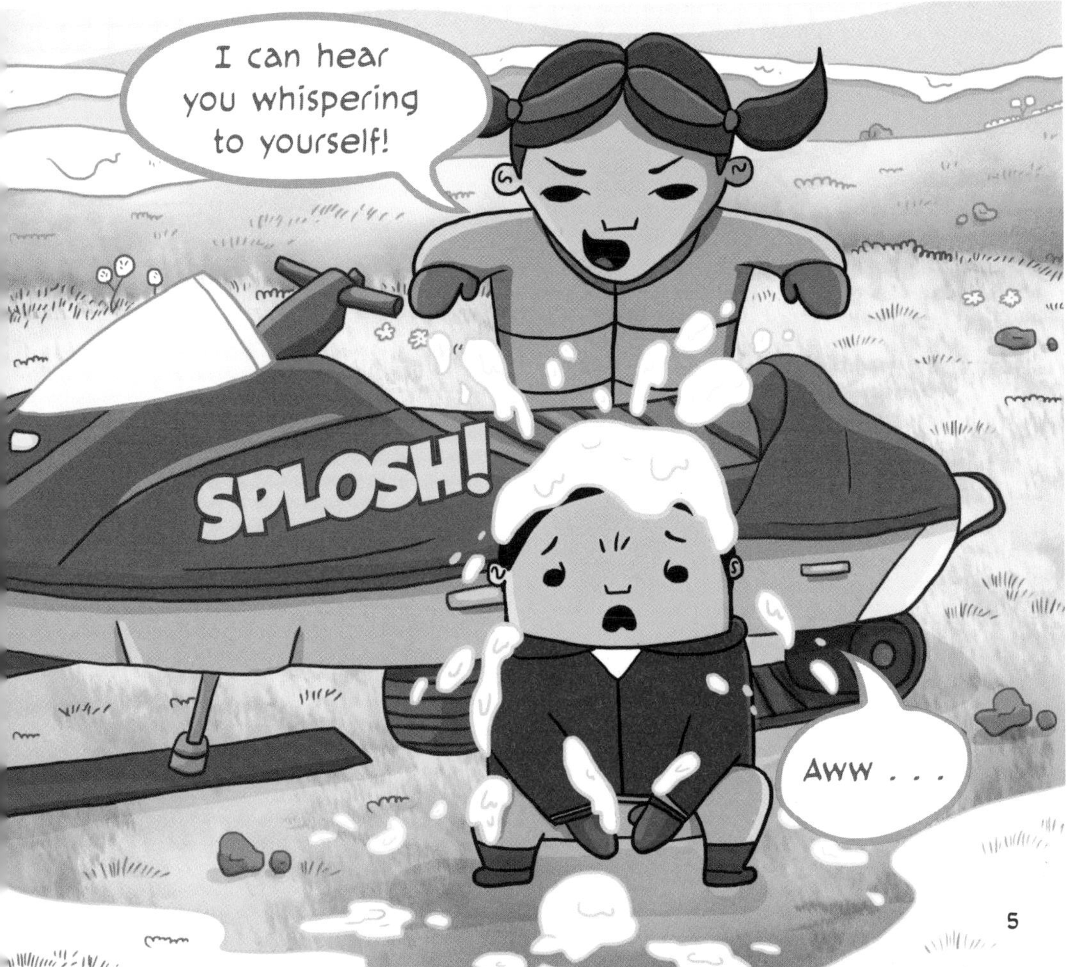
I can hear you whispering to yourself!
SPLOSH!
AWW . . .

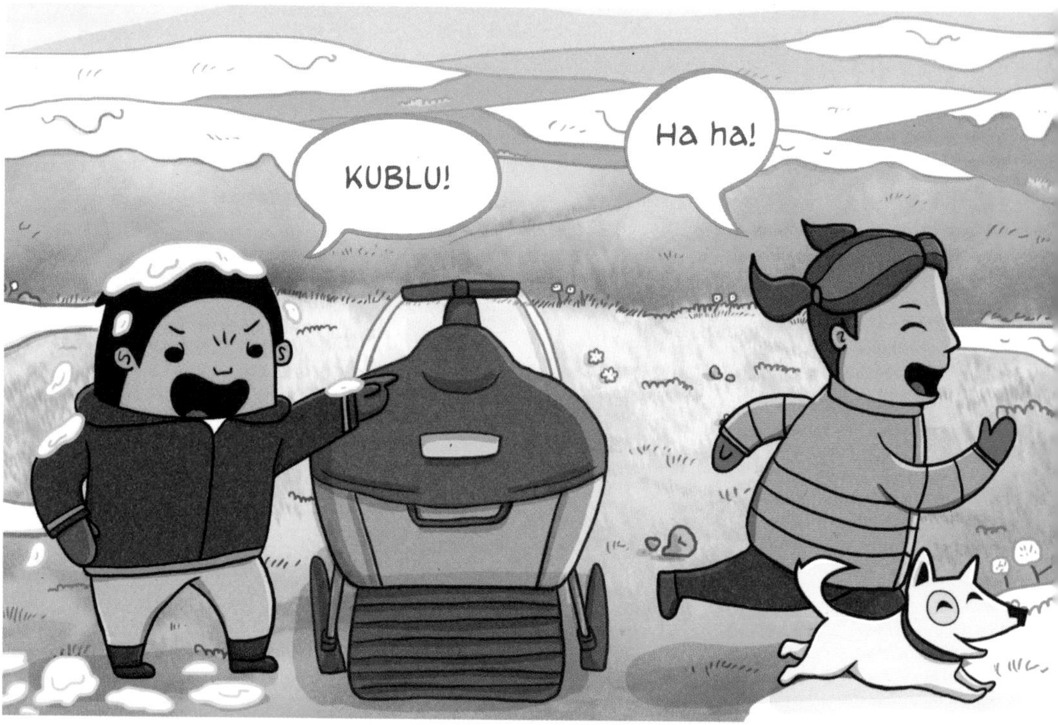
KUBLU!
Ha ha!

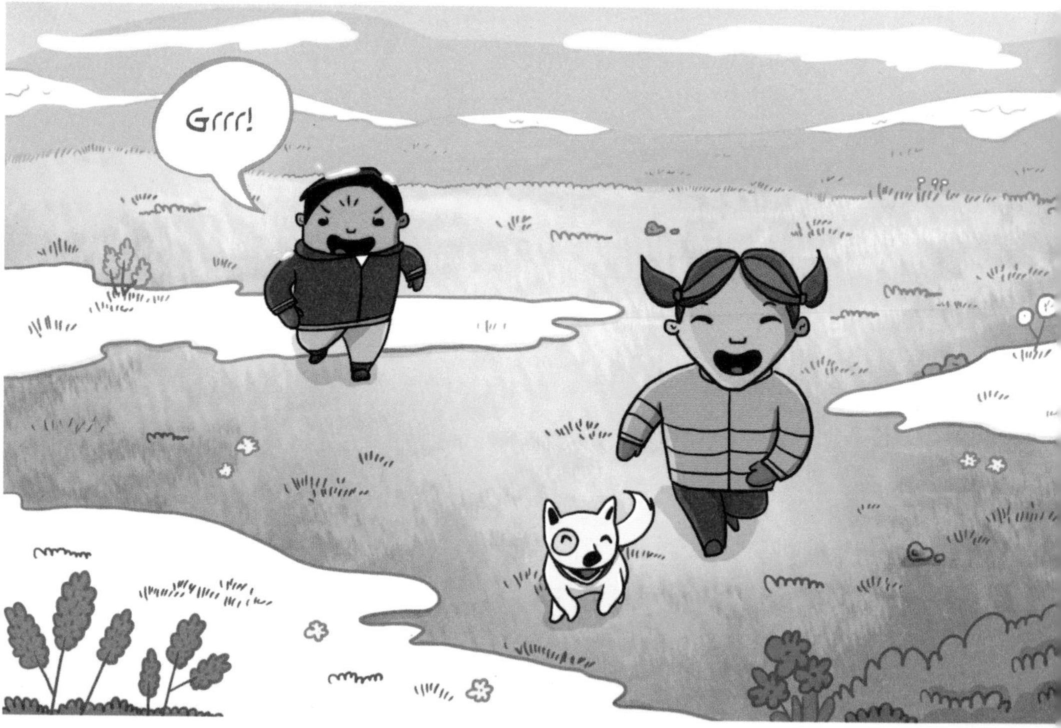
Grrr!

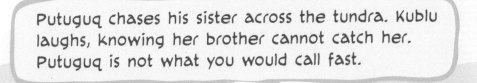

Putuguq chases his sister across the tundra. Kublu laughs, knowing her brother cannot catch her. Putuguq is not what you would call fast.

Not fair! Your legs are longer than mine.

You'll never catch me!

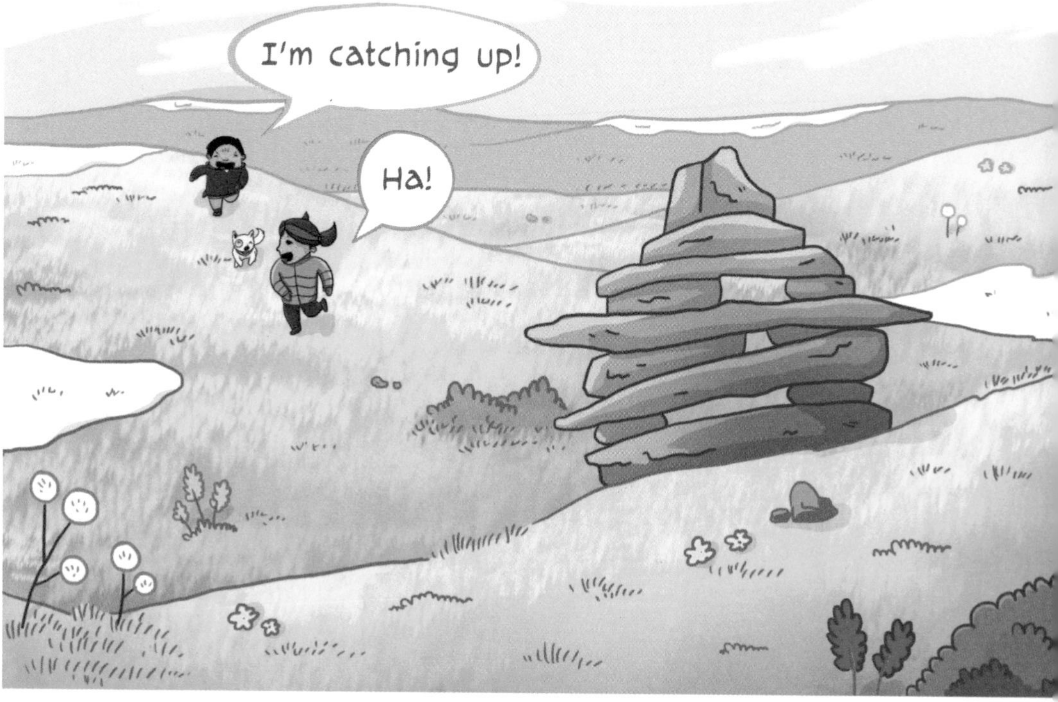
I'm catching up!
Ha!

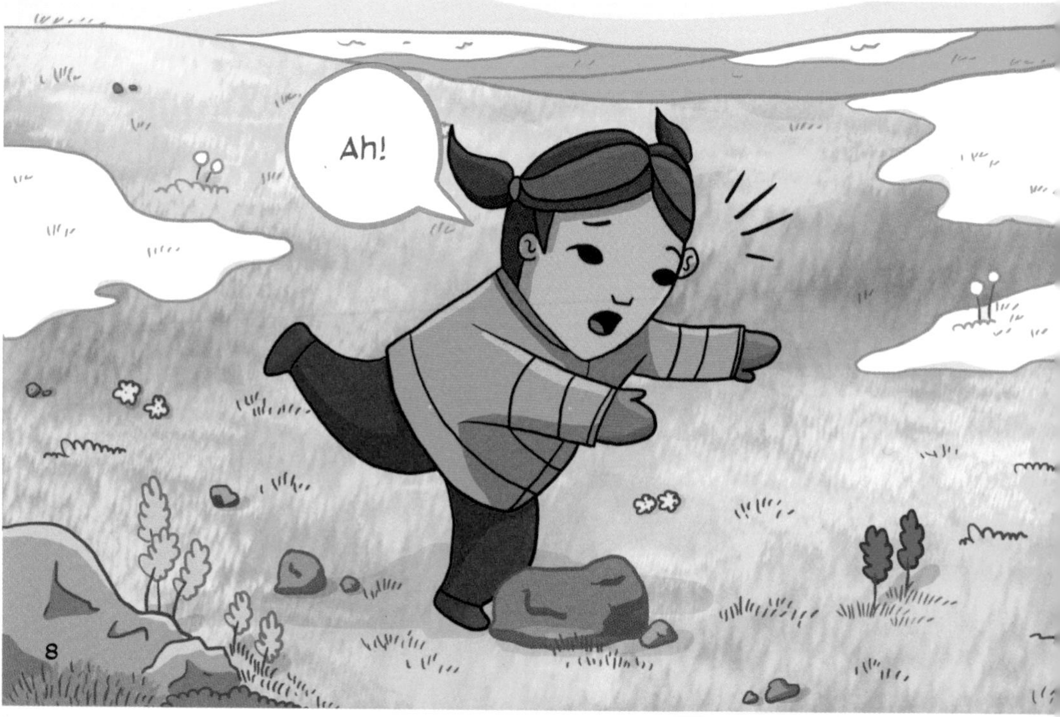
Ah!

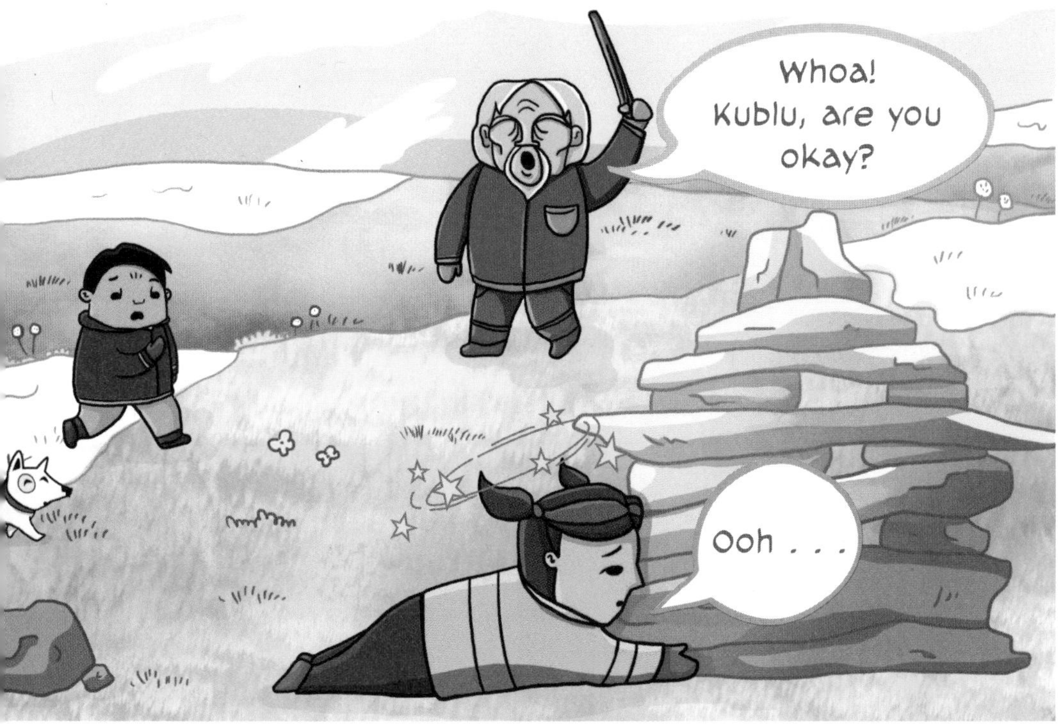
Whoa! Kublu, are you okay?
Ooh . . .

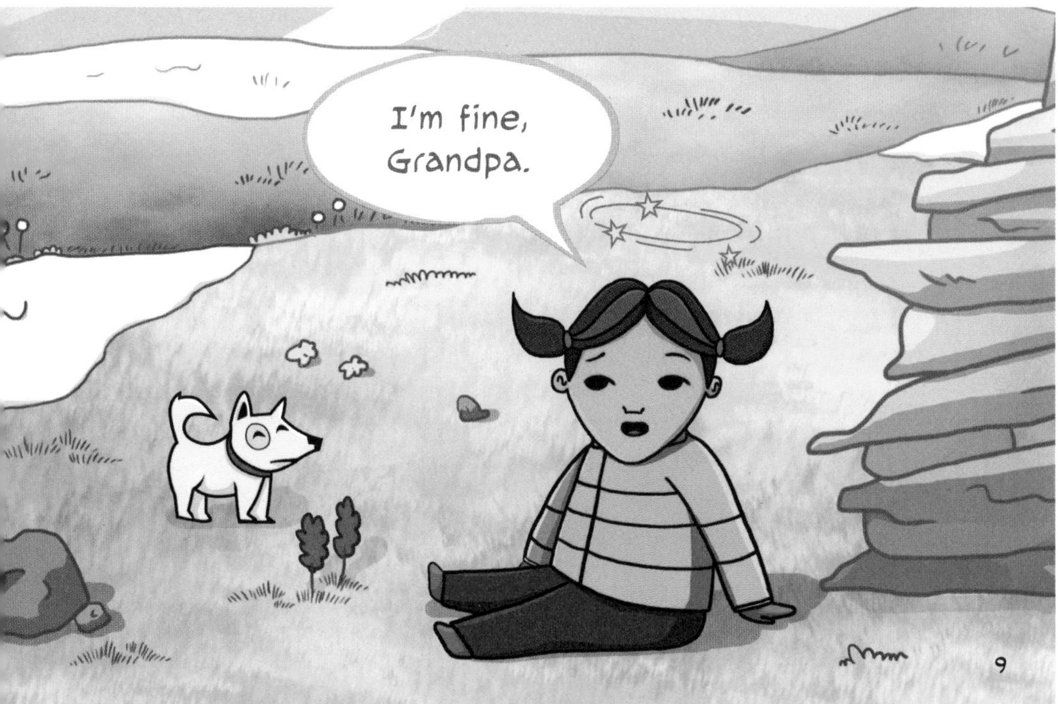
I'm fine, Grandpa.

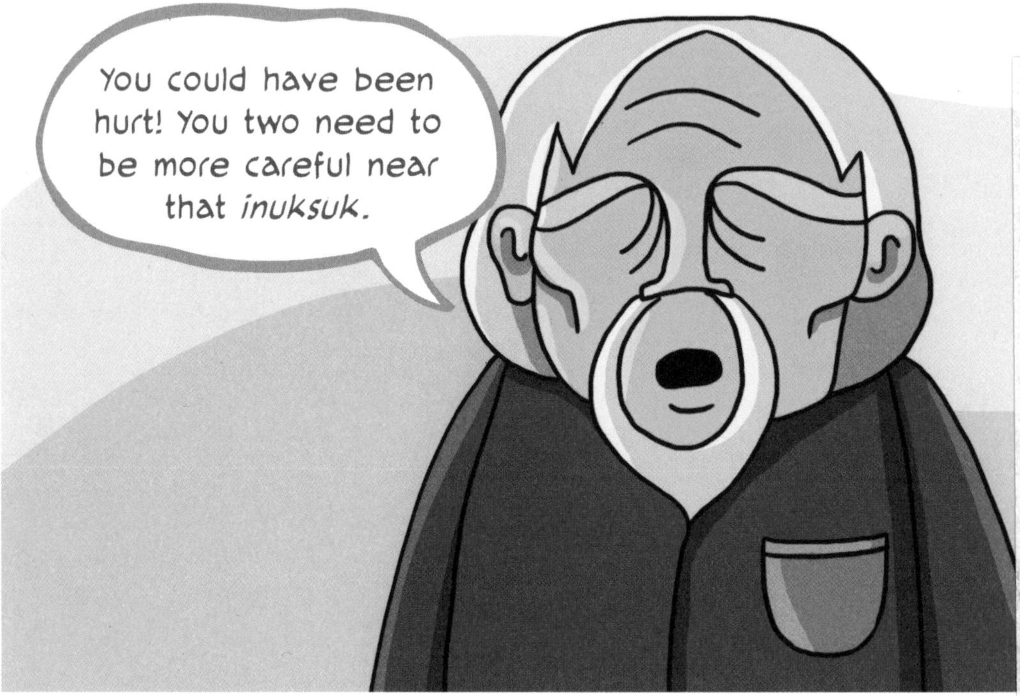
You could have been hurt! You two need to be more careful near that *inuksuk*.

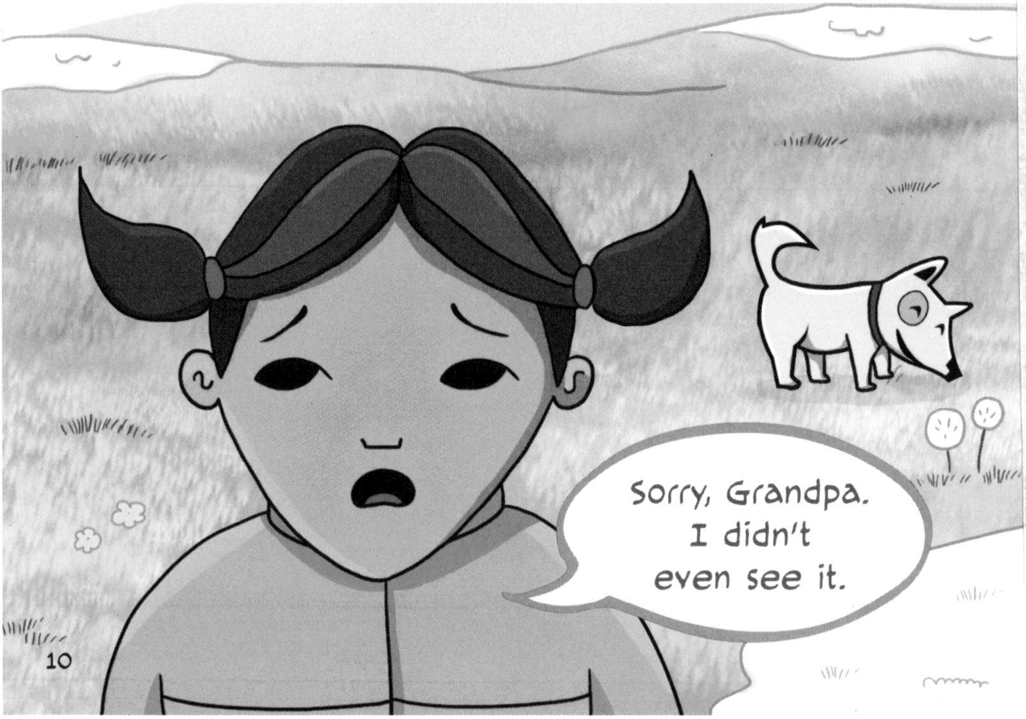
Sorry, Grandpa. I didn't even see it.

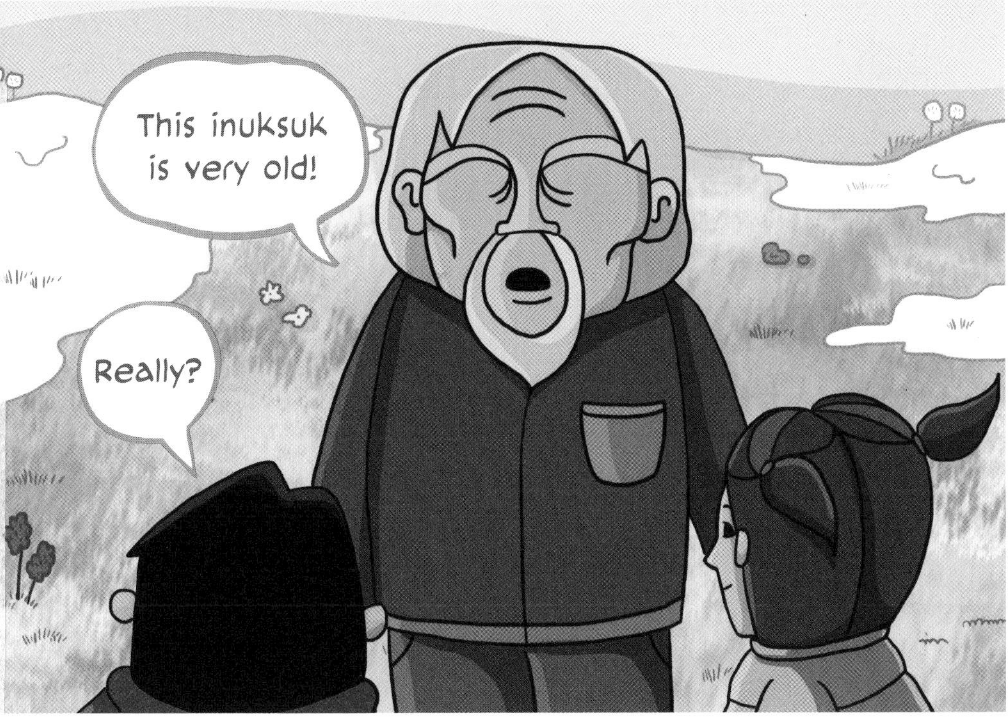
This inuksuk is very old!
Really?

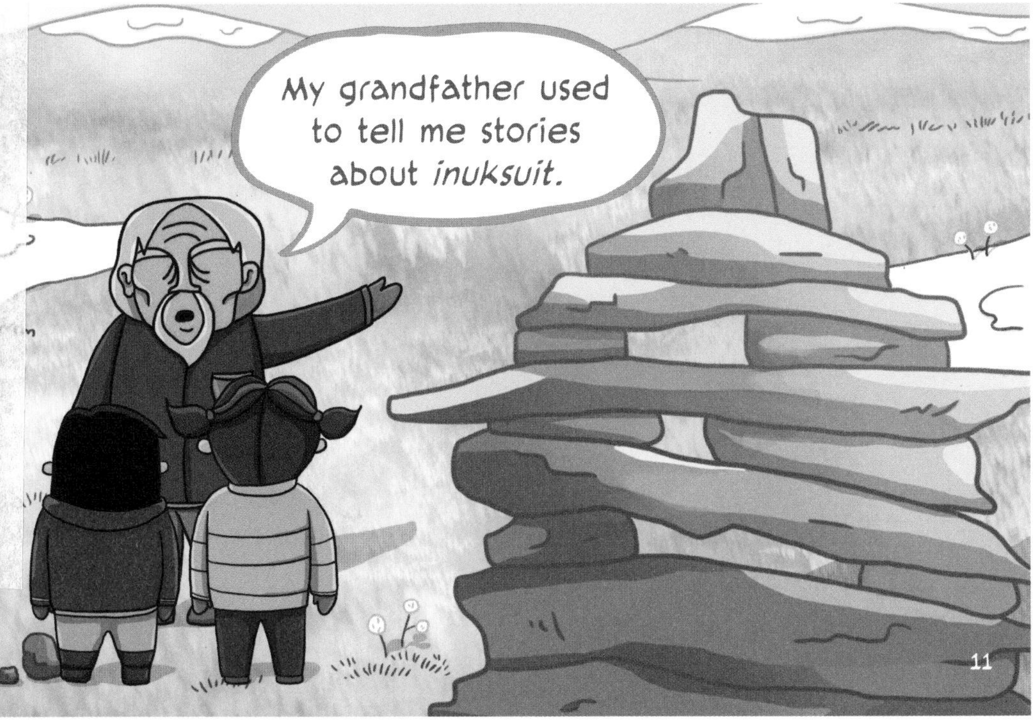
My grandfather used to tell me stories about *inuksuit*.

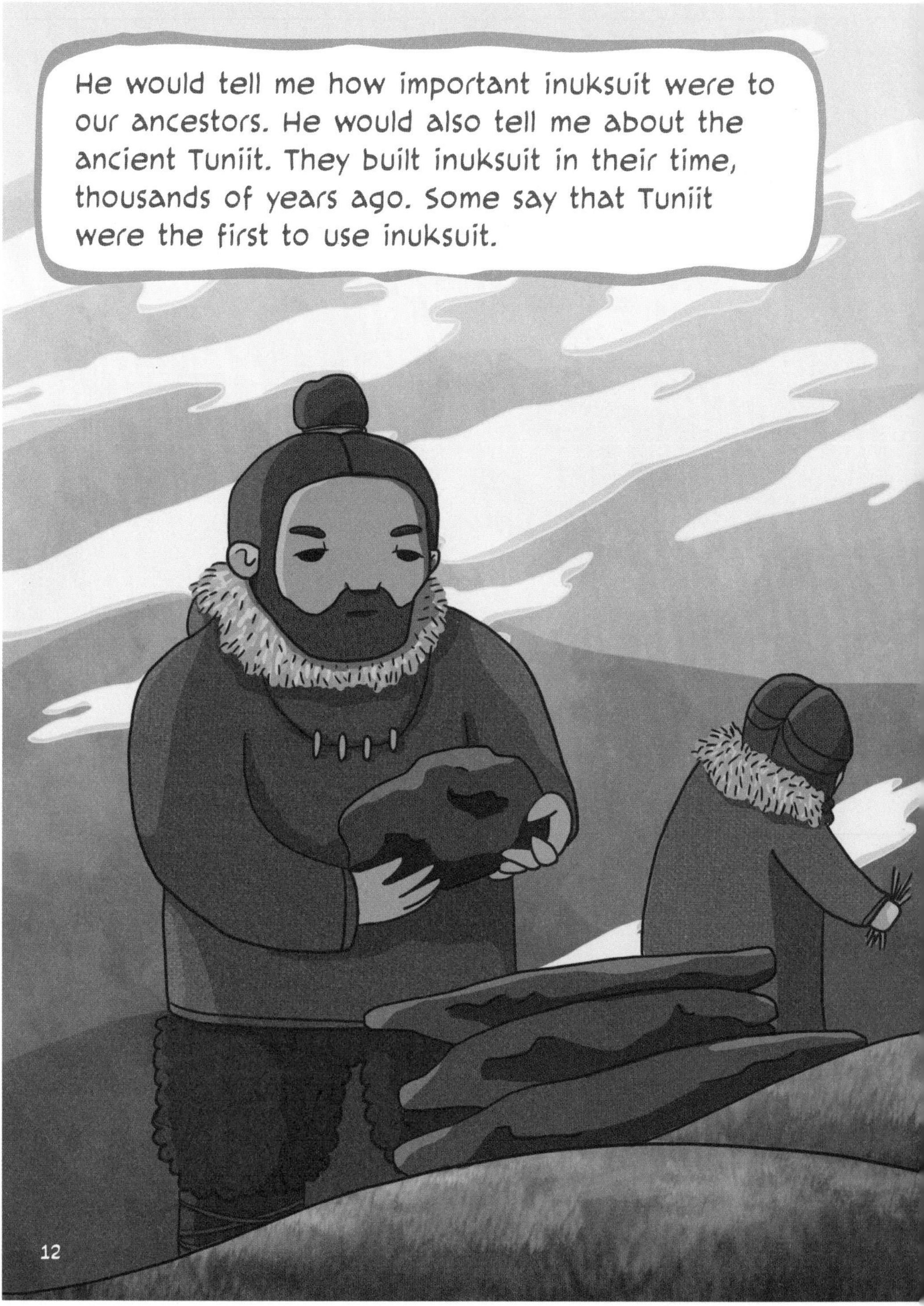
He would tell me how important inuksuit were to our ancestors. He would also tell me about the ancient Tuniit. They built inuksuit in their time, thousands of years ago. Some say that Tuniit were the first to use inuksuit.

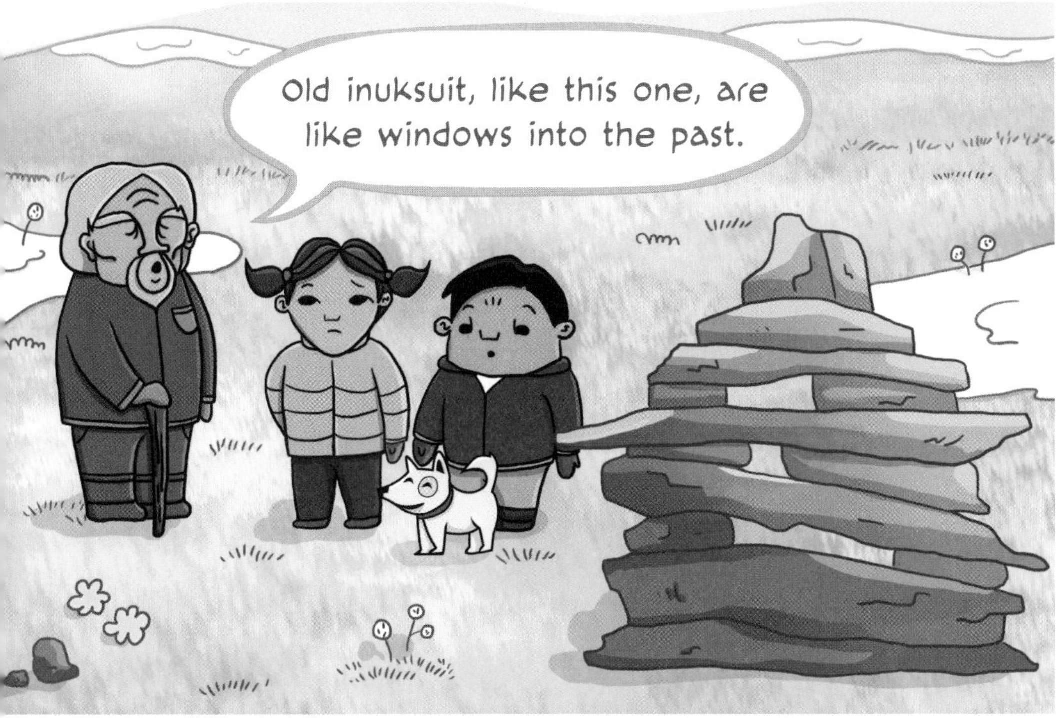
Old inuksuit, like this one, are like windows into the past.

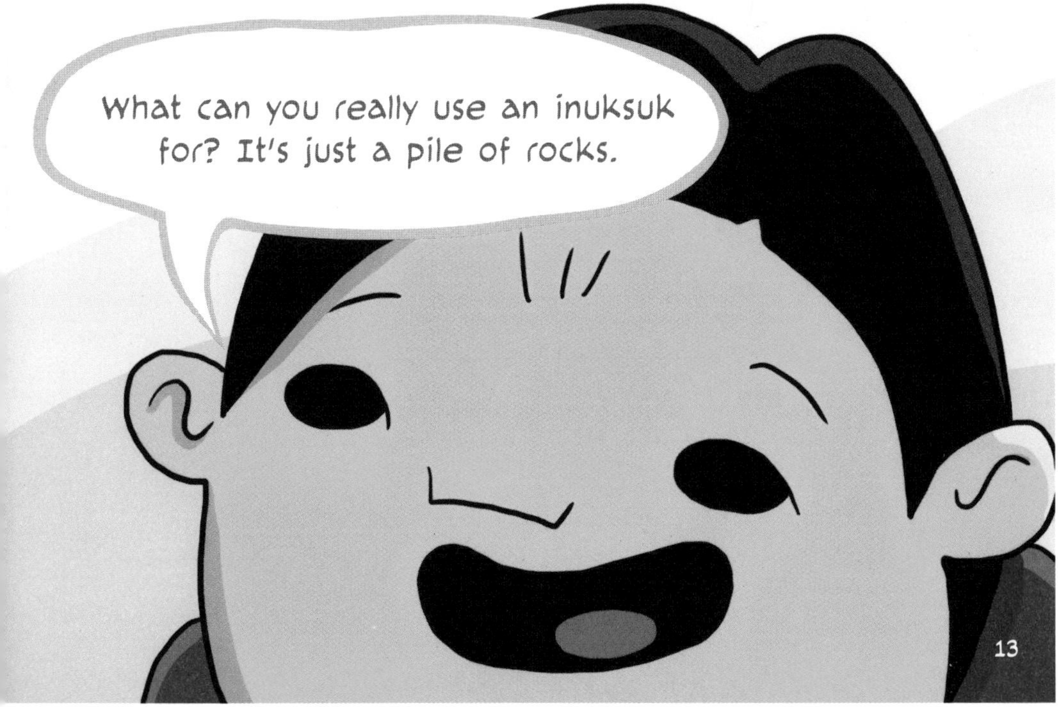
What can you really use an inuksuk for? It's just a pile of rocks.

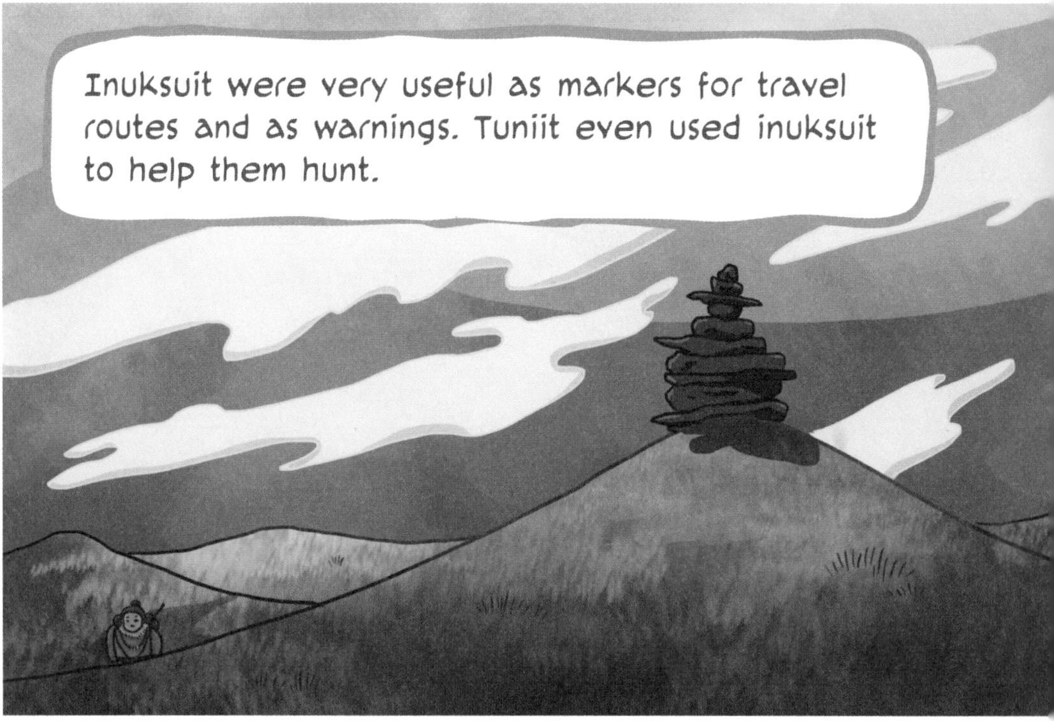
Inuksuit were very useful as markers for travel routes and as warnings. Tuniit even used inuksuit to help them hunt.

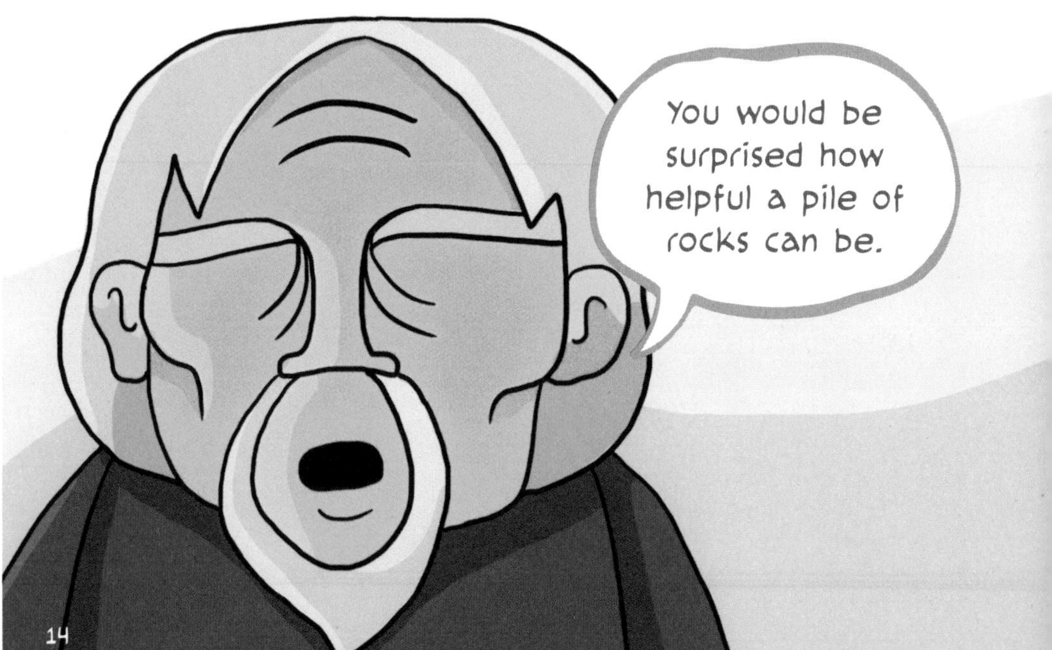
You would be surprised how helpful a pile of rocks can be.

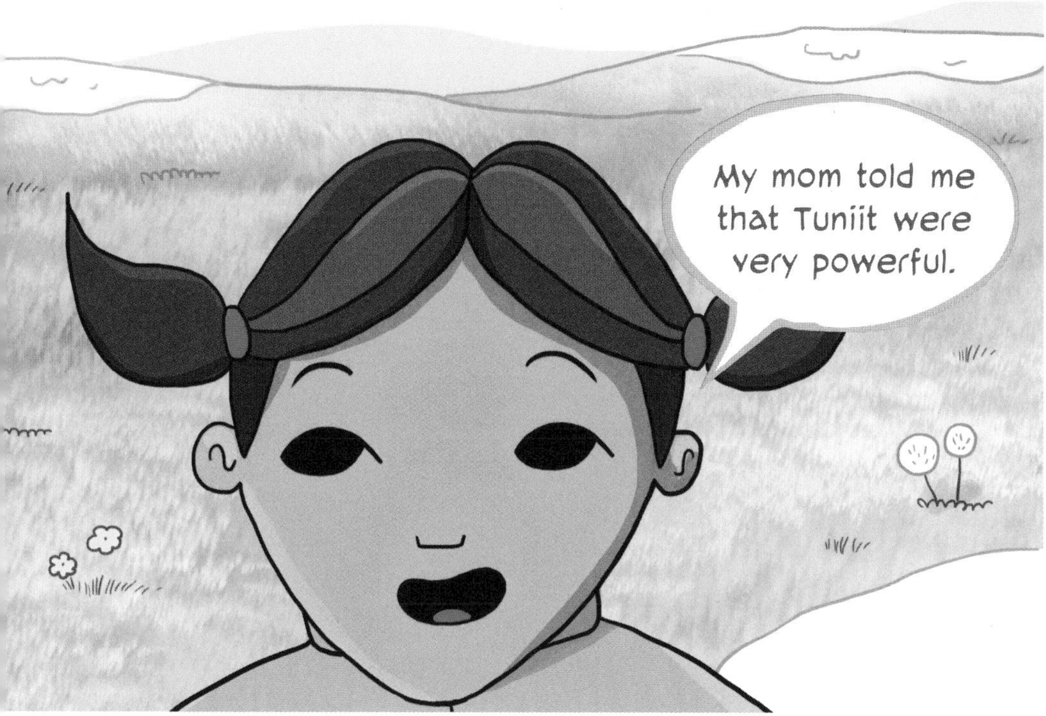
My mom told me that Tuniit were very powerful.

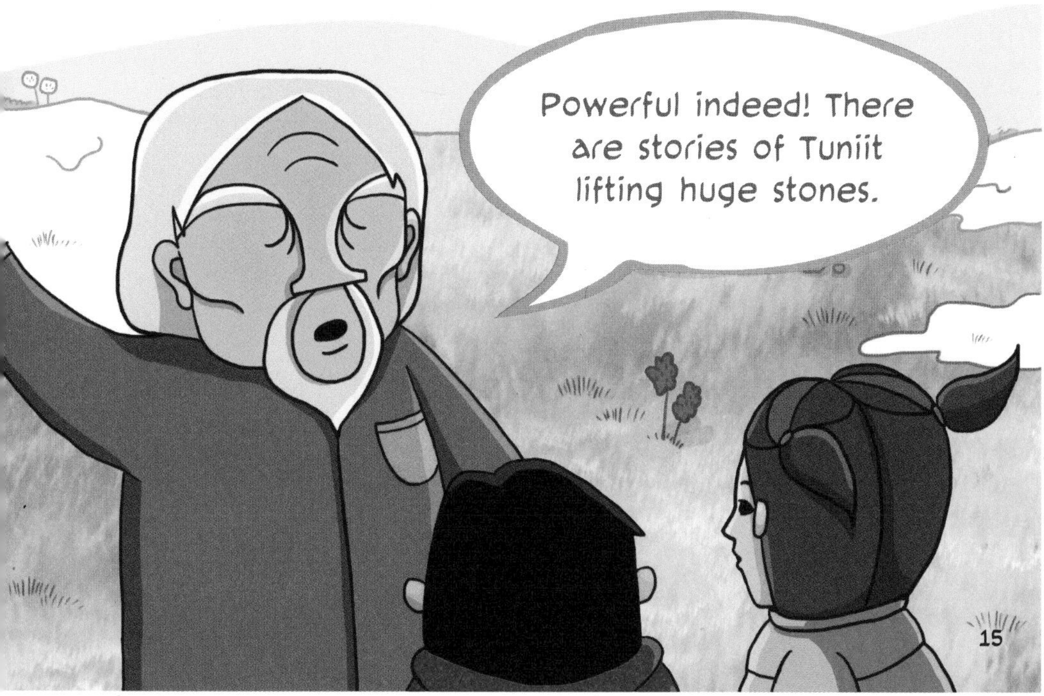
Powerful indeed! There are stories of Tuniit lifting huge stones.

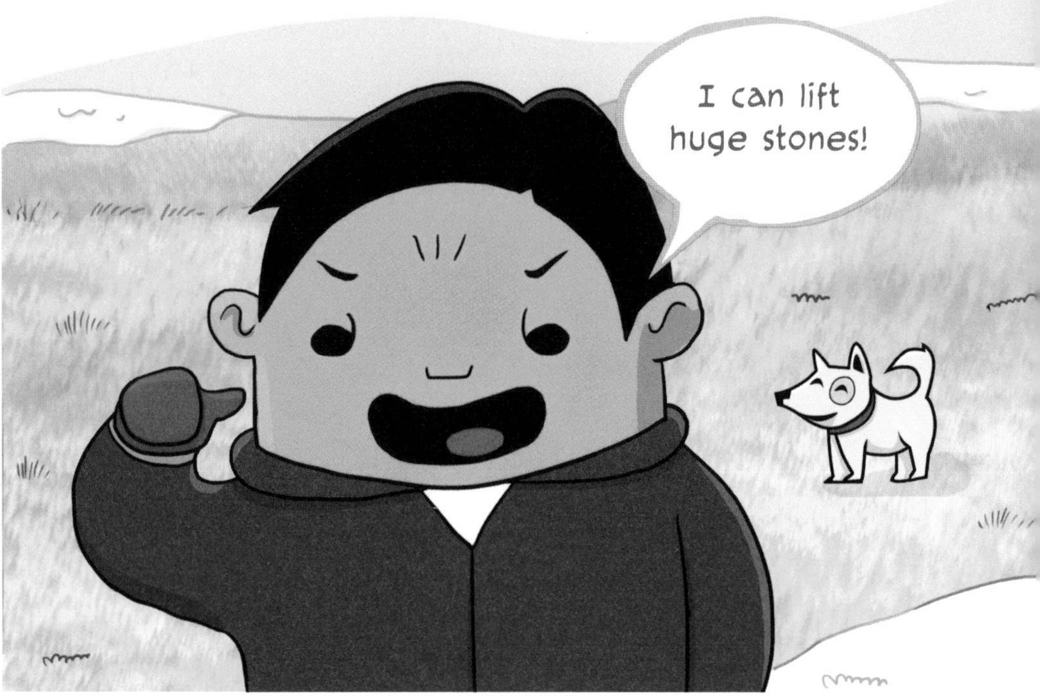
I can lift huge stones!

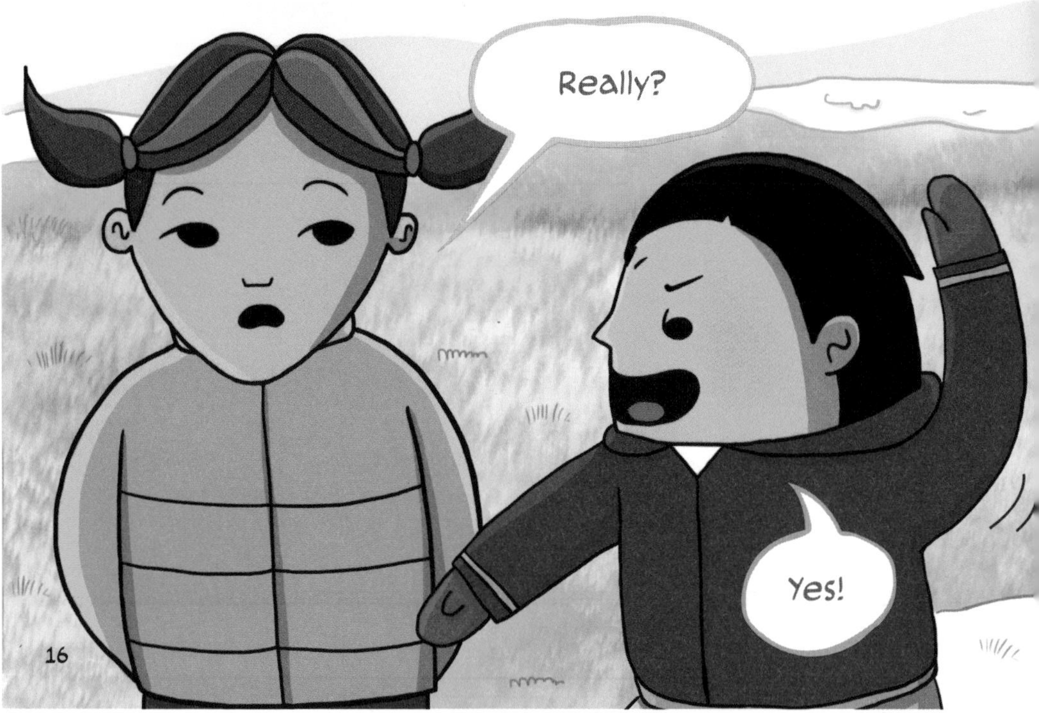
Really?
Yes!

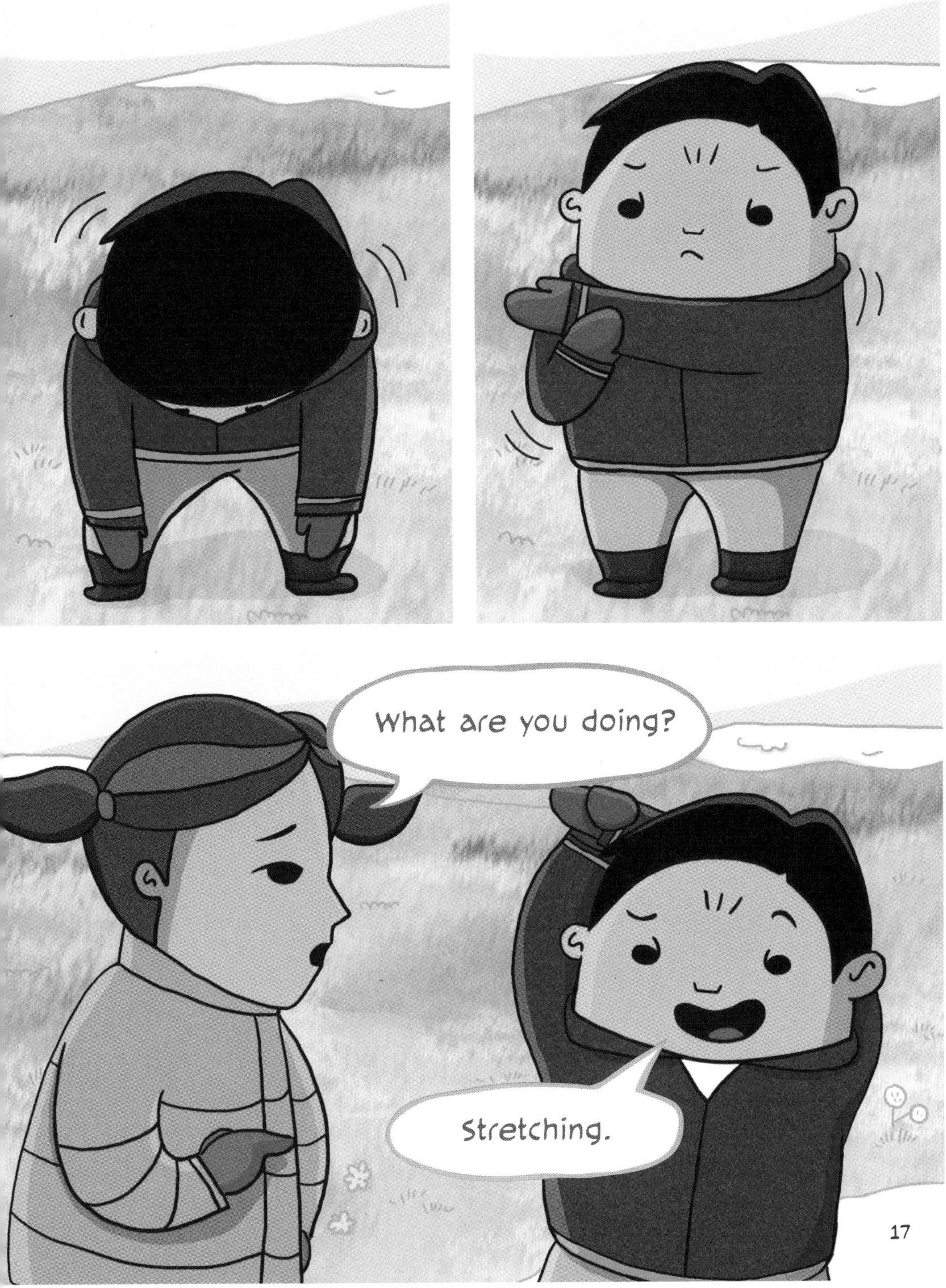
What are you doing?
Stretching.

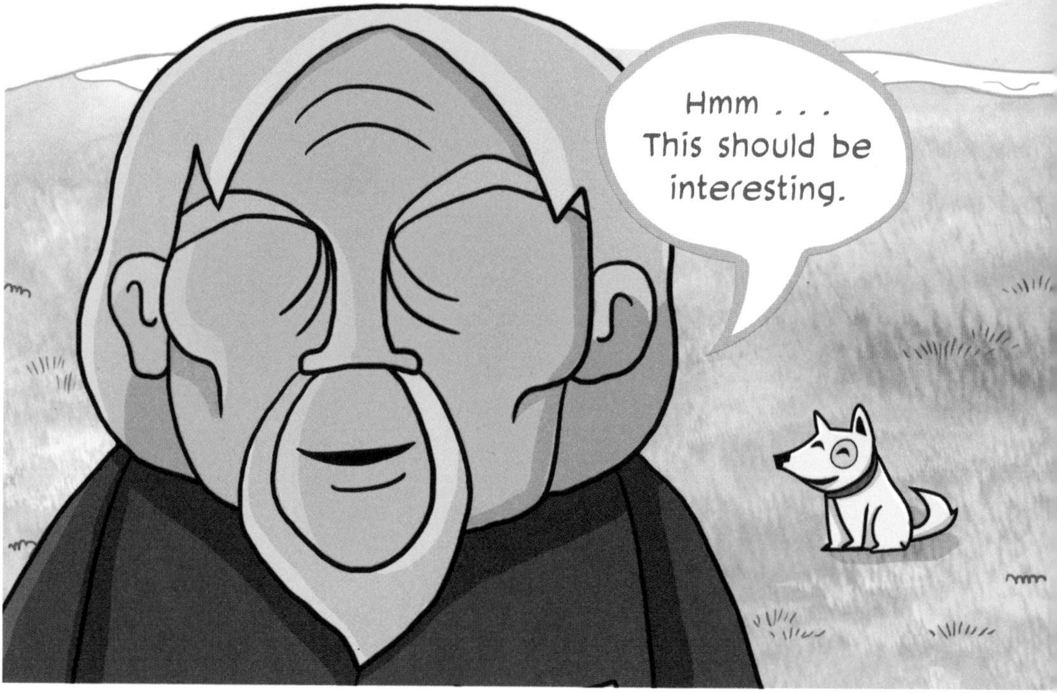
Hmm . . . This should be interesting.

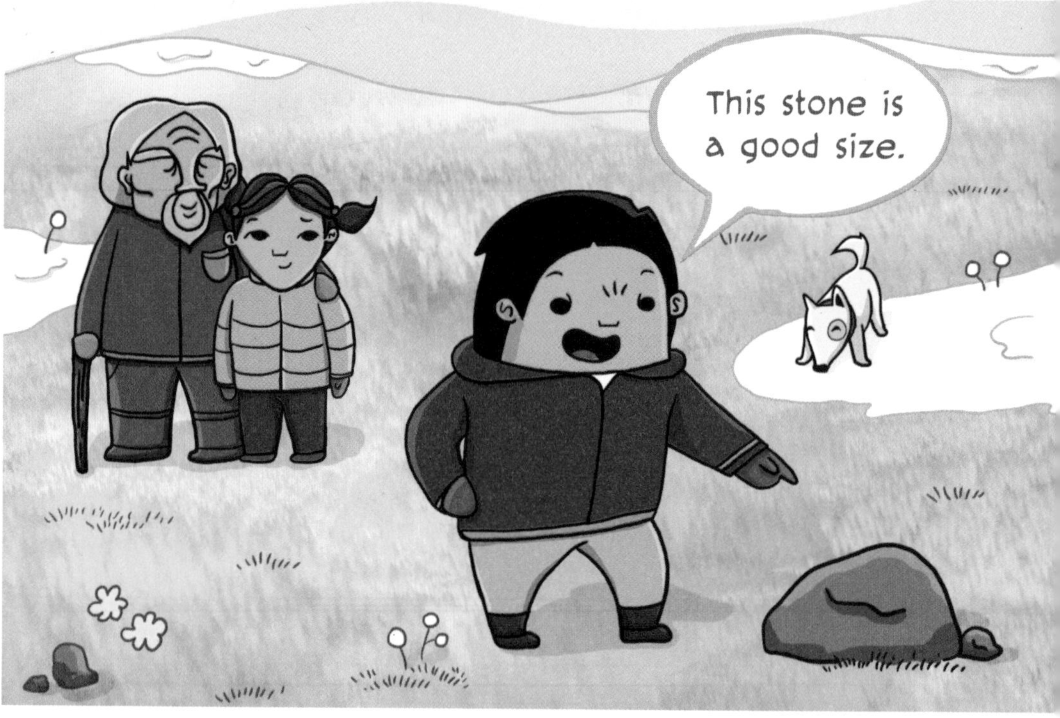
This stone is a good size.

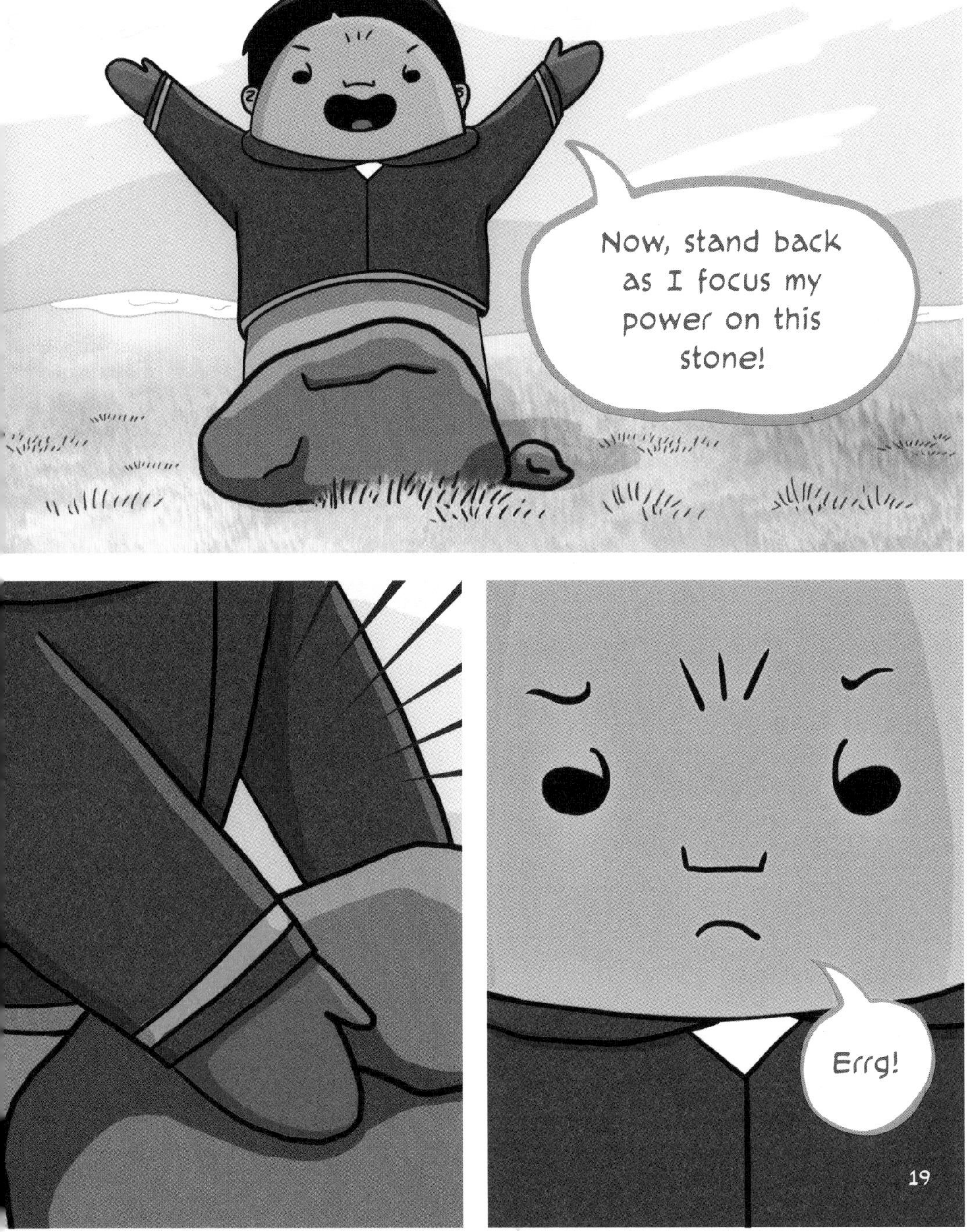
Now, stand back as I focus my power on this stone!
Errg!

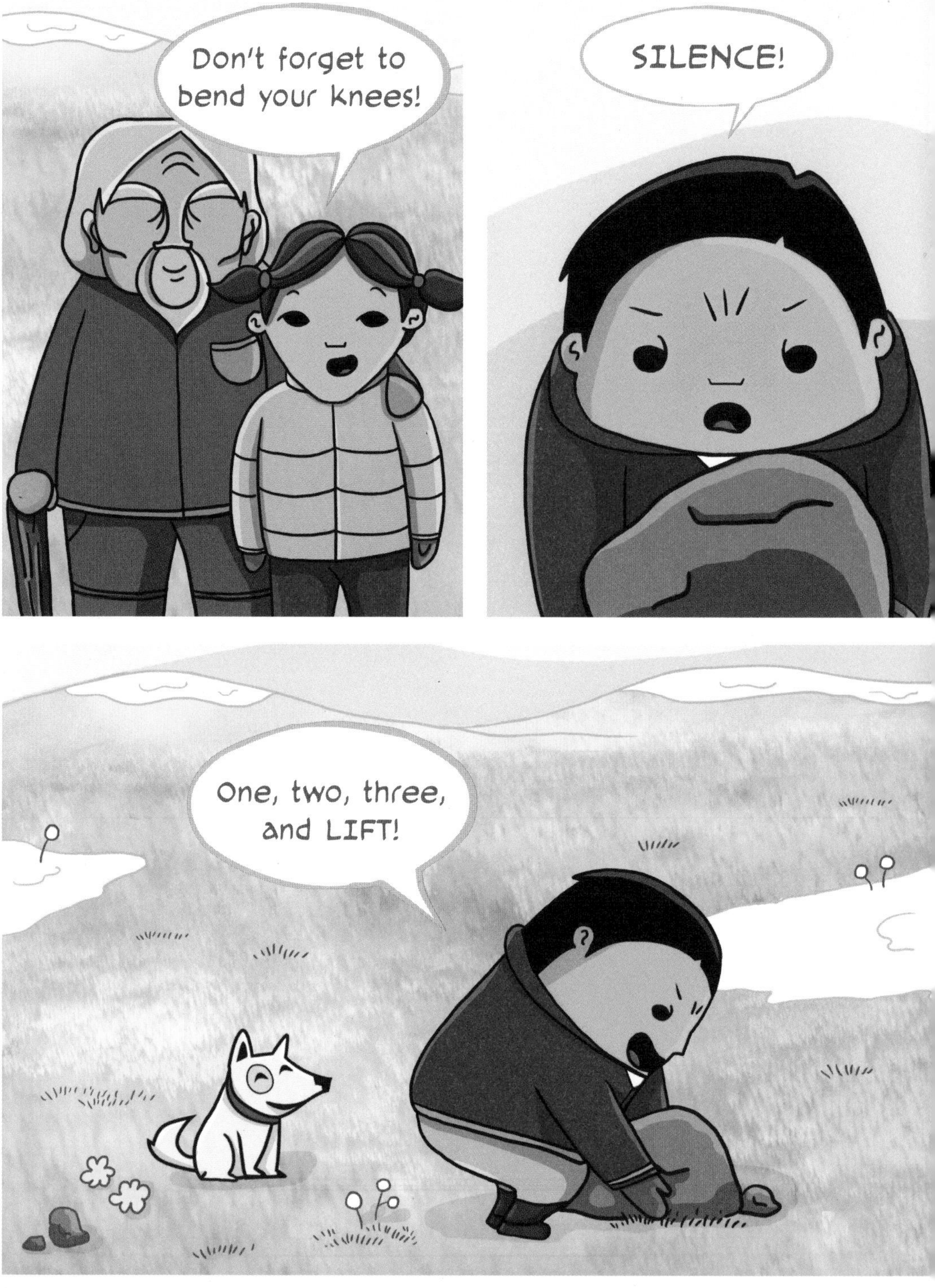
Don't forget to bend your knees!
SILENCE!
One, two, three, and LIFT!

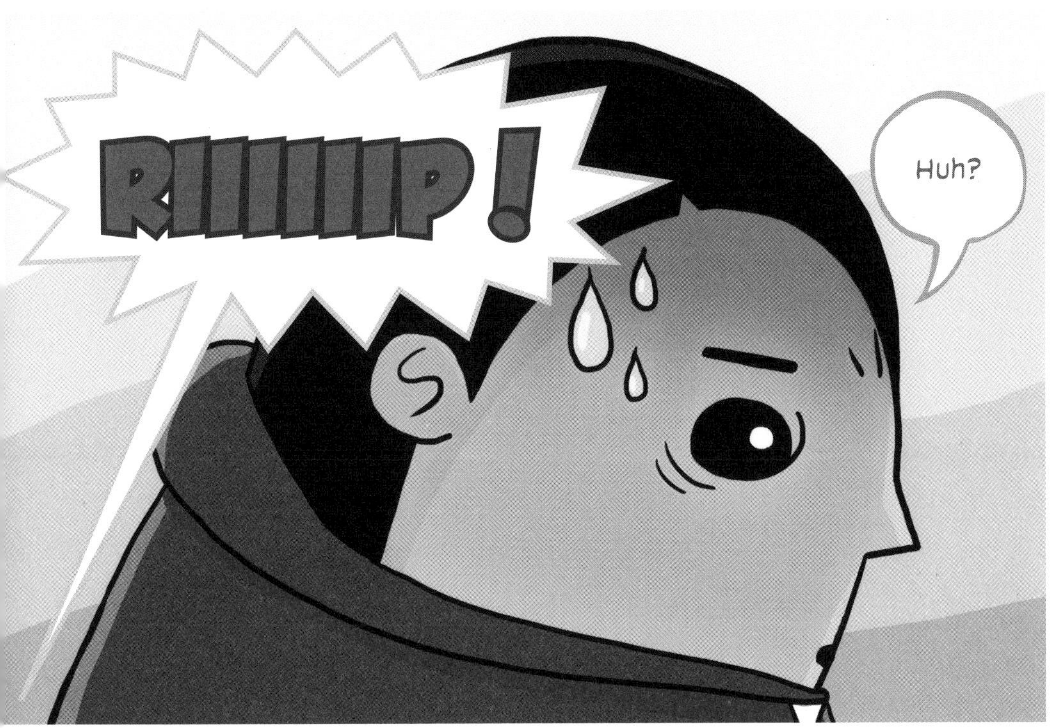
RIIIIIIP!
Huh?

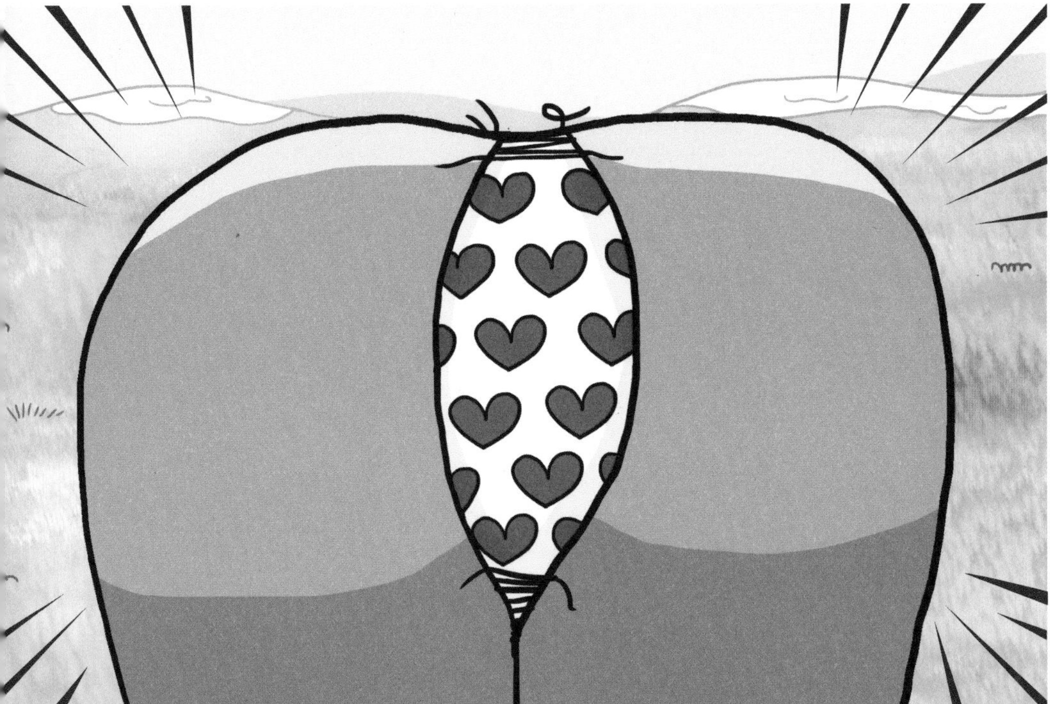

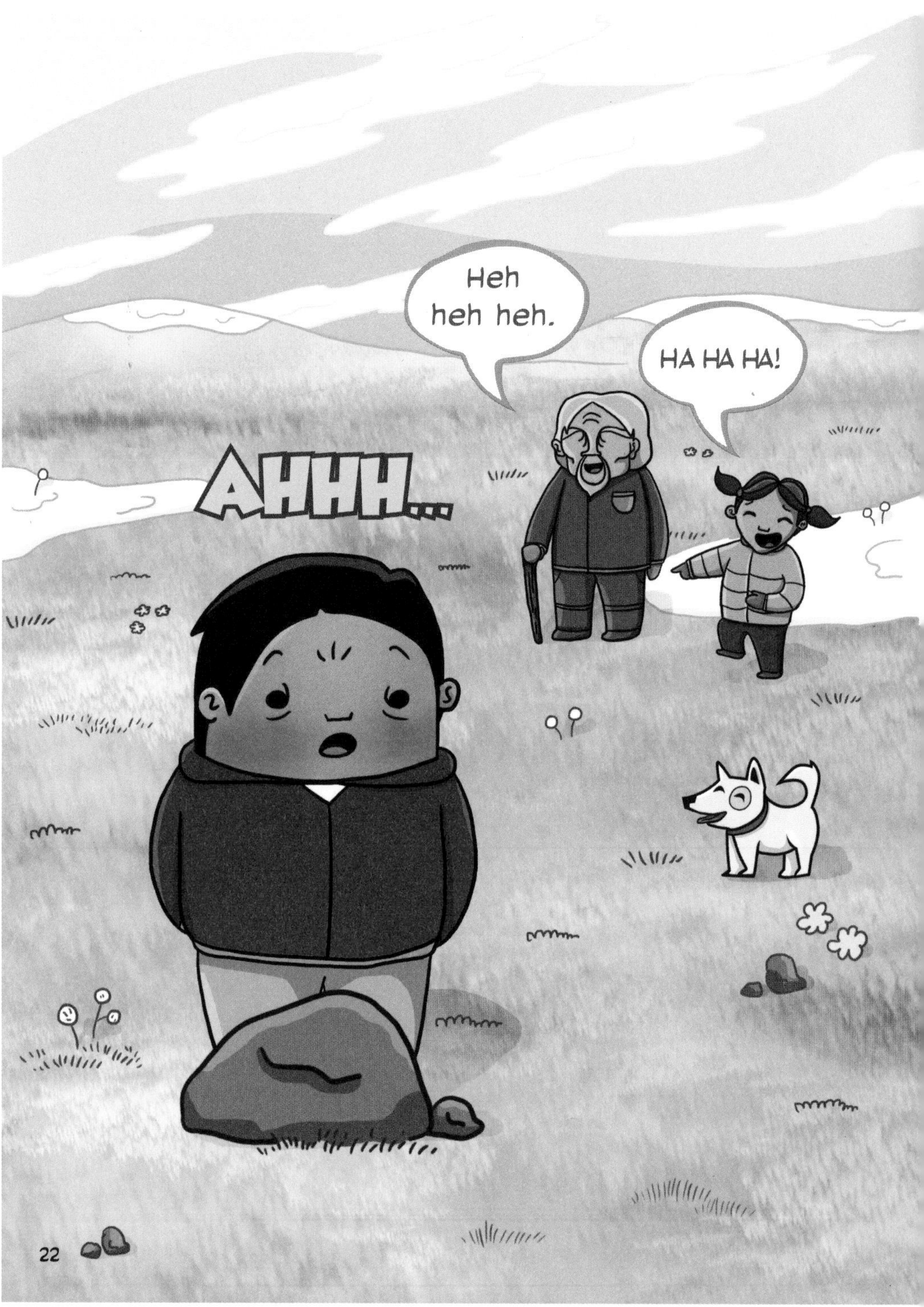
Heh
heh heh.
HA HA HA!
AHHH...

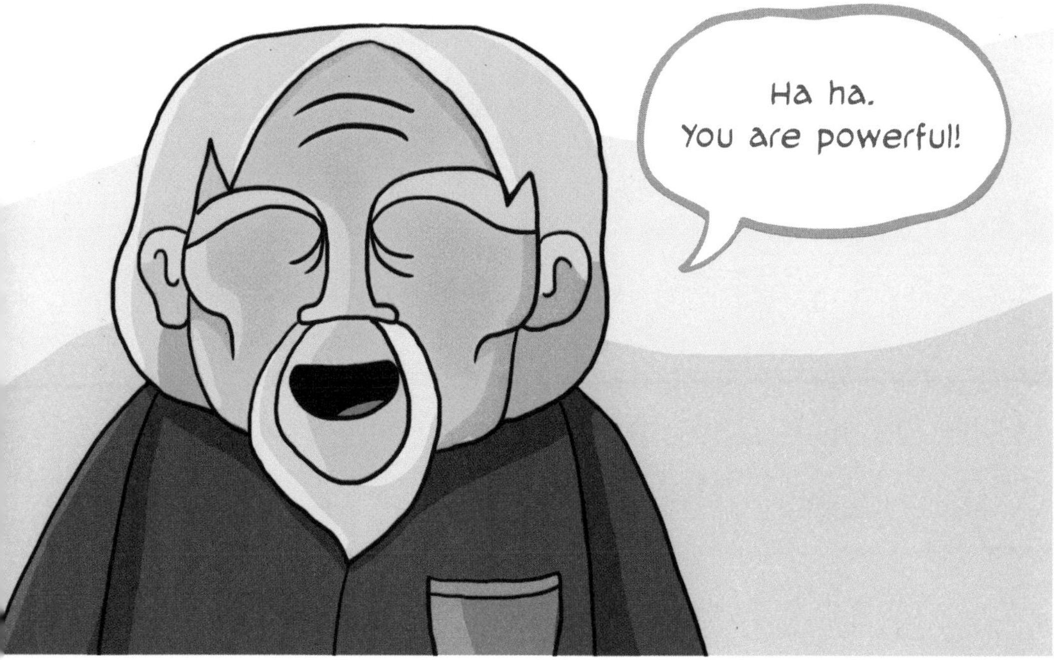
Ha ha.
You are powerful!

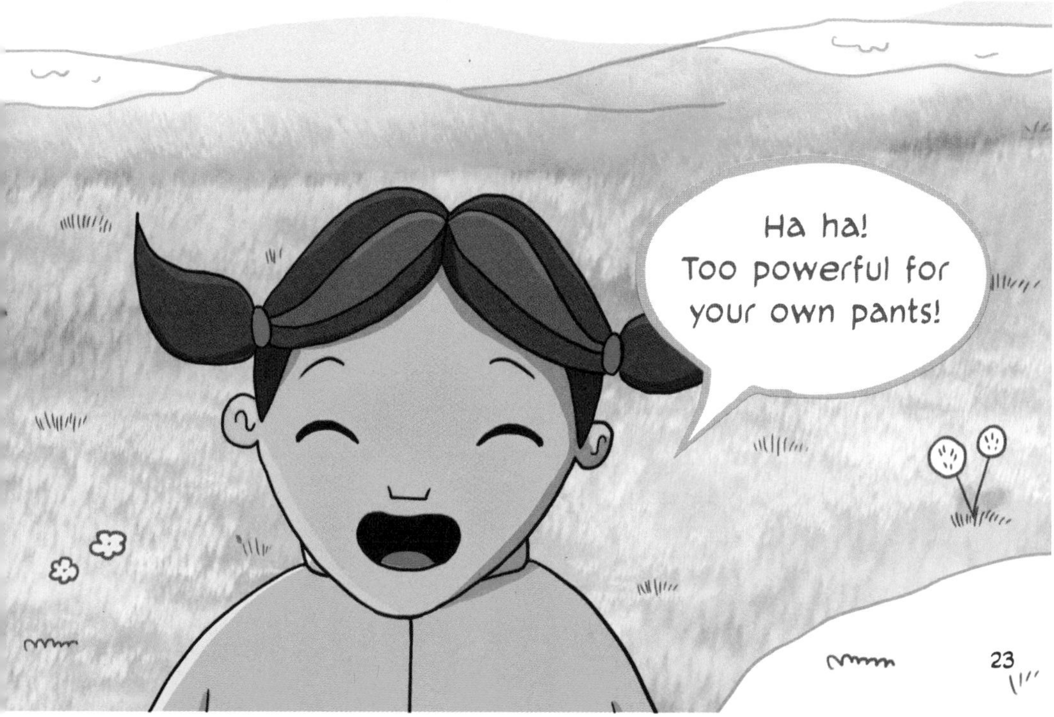
Ha ha!
Too powerful for
your own pants!

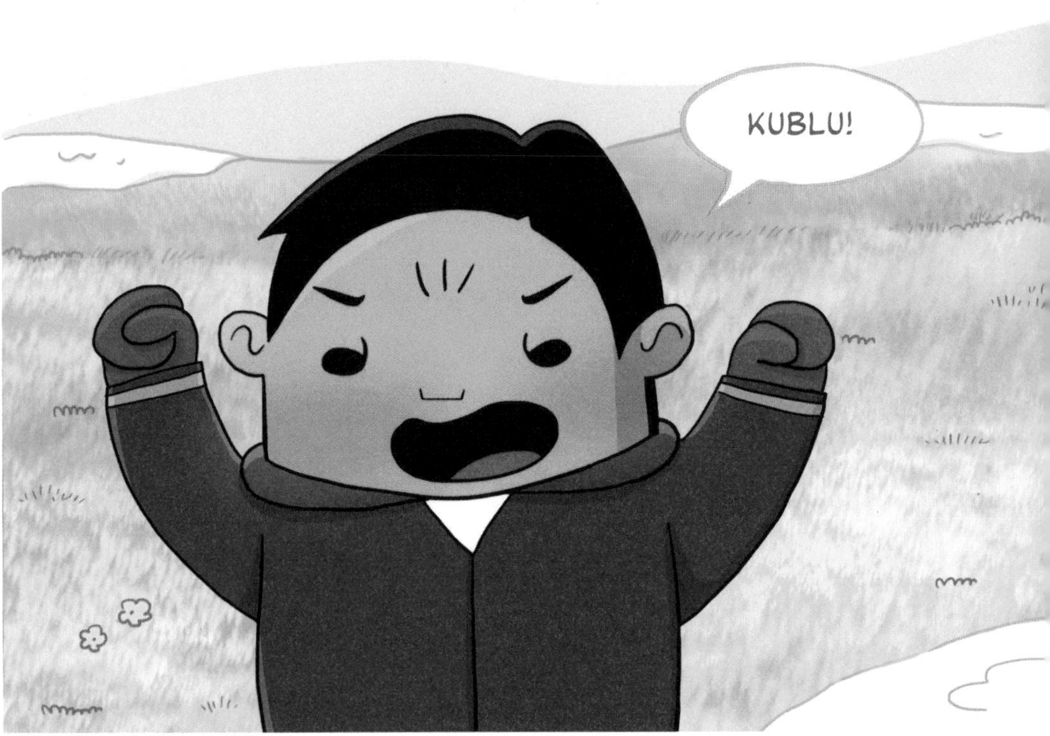
KUBLU!

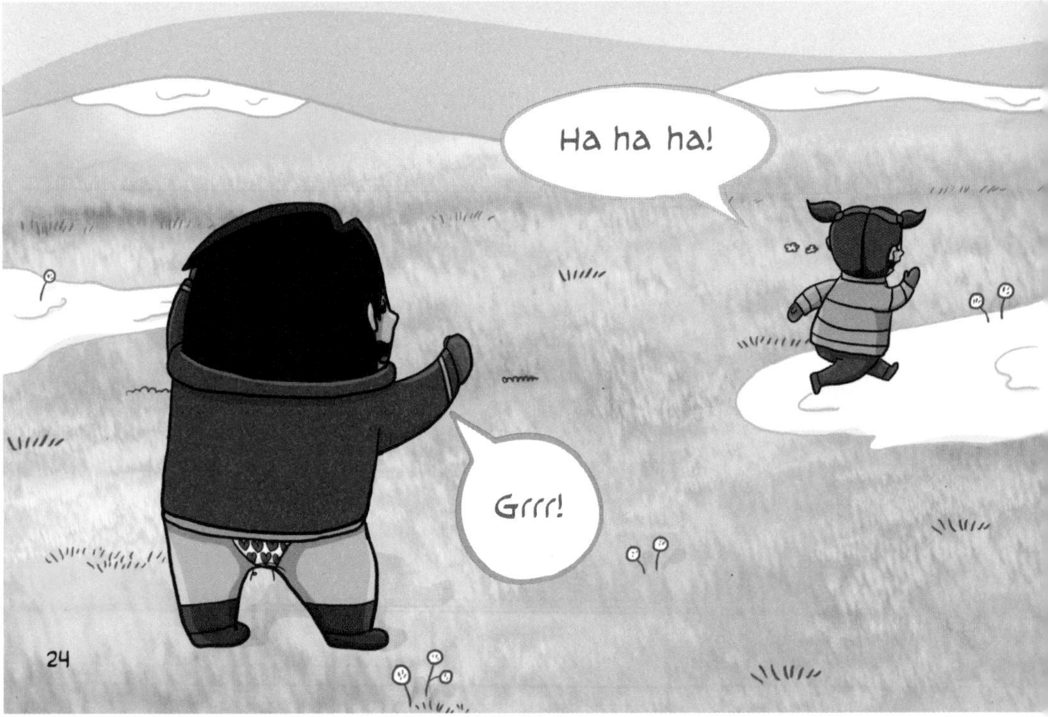
Ha ha ha!
Grrr!

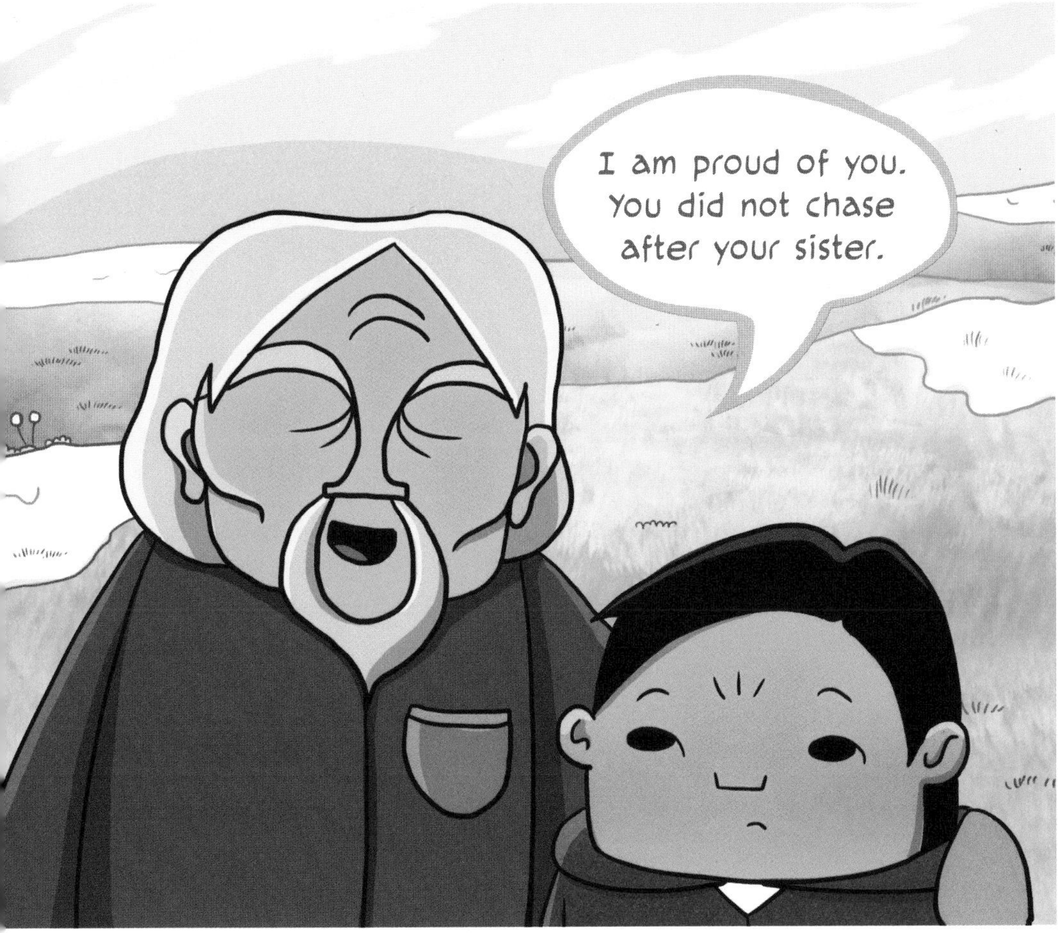
I am proud of you. You did not chase after your sister.

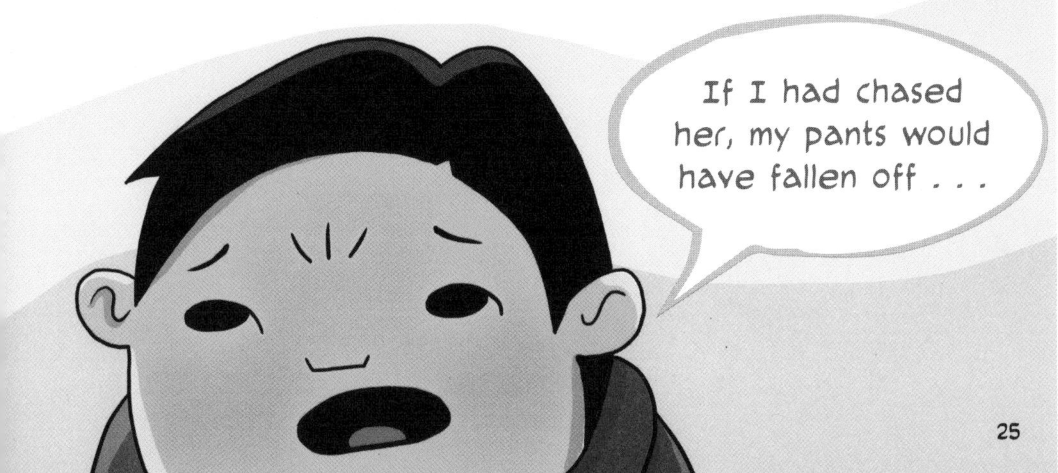
If I had chased her, my pants would have fallen off . . .

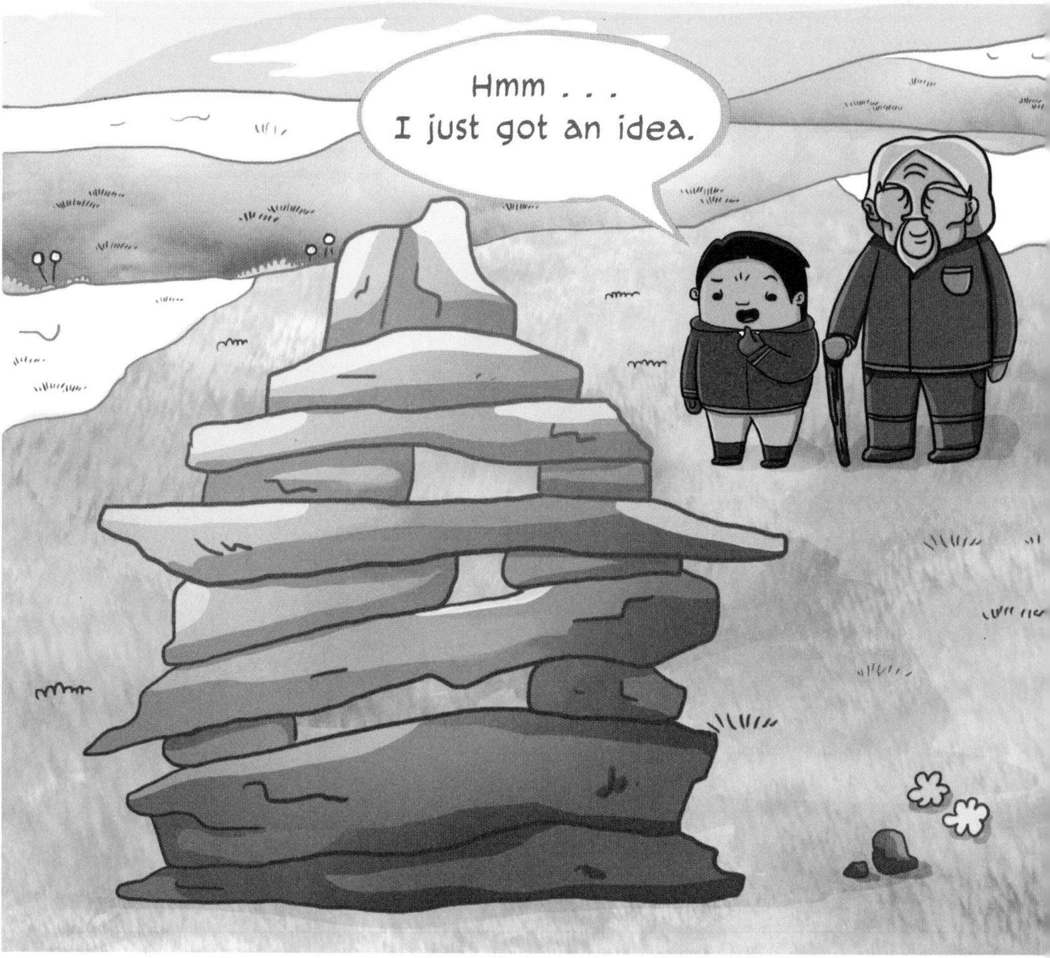
Hmm . . .
I just got an idea.

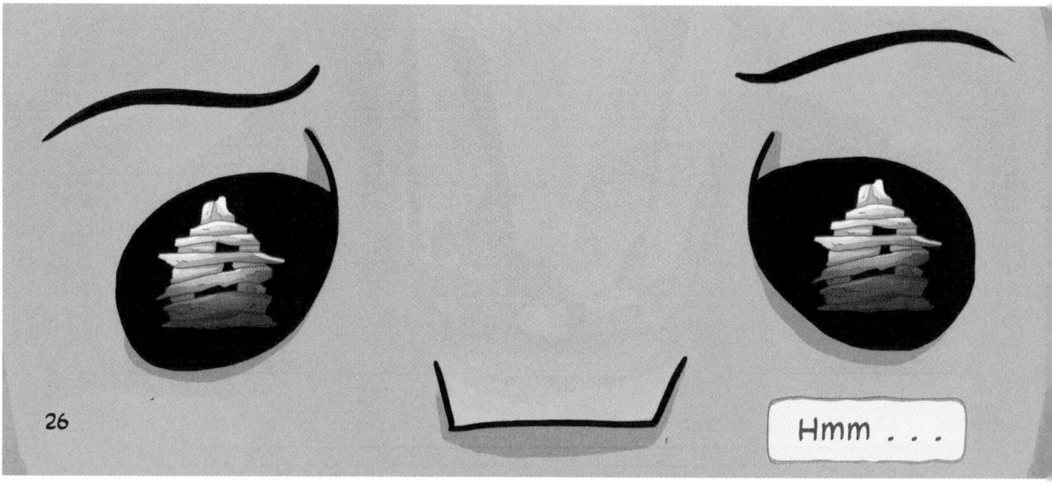
Hmm . . .

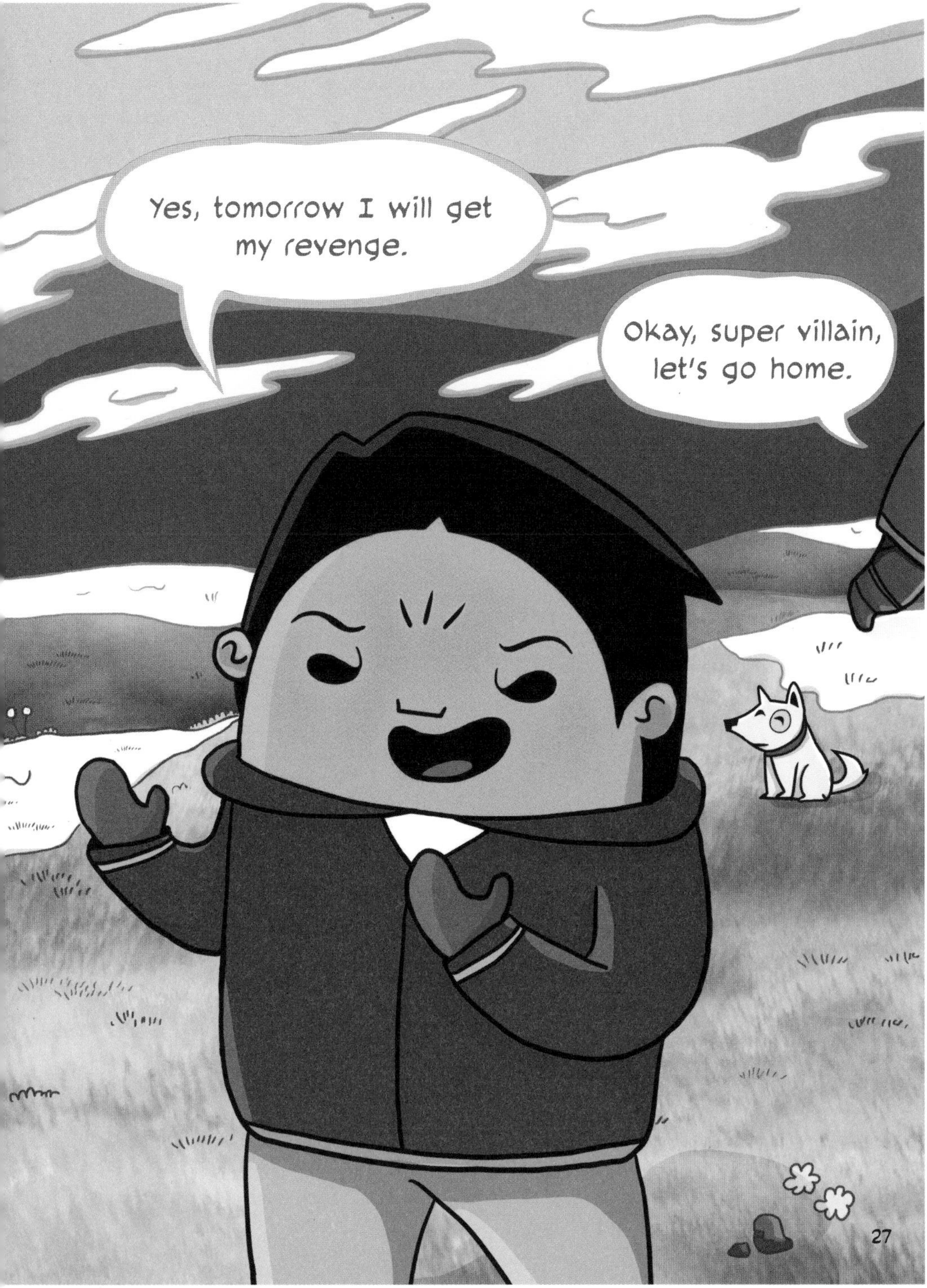
Yes, tomorrow I will get my revenge.
Okay, super villain, let's go home.

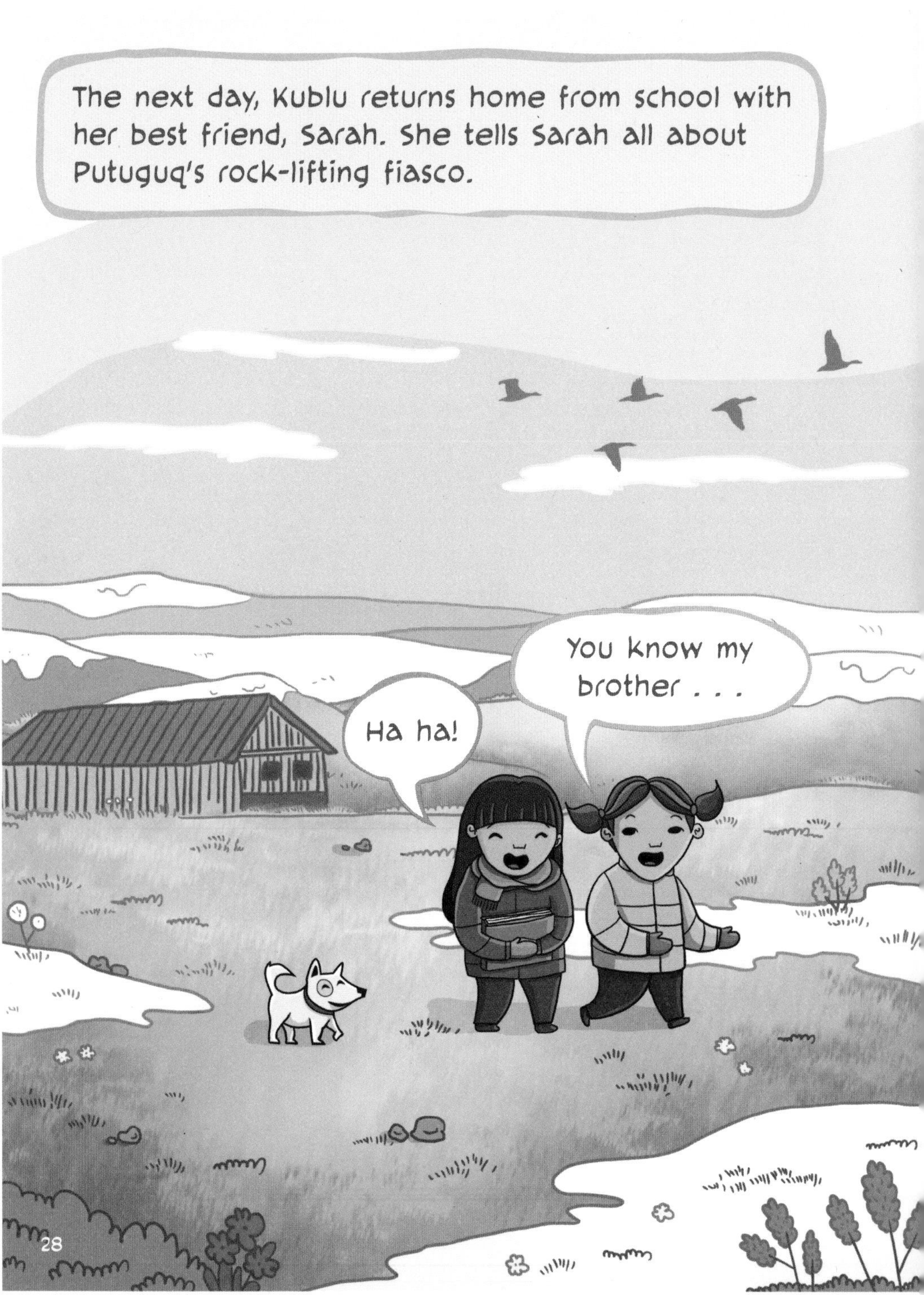
The next day, Kublu returns home from school with her best friend, Sarah. She tells Sarah all about Putuguq's rock-lifting fiasco.
Ha ha!
You know my brother . . .

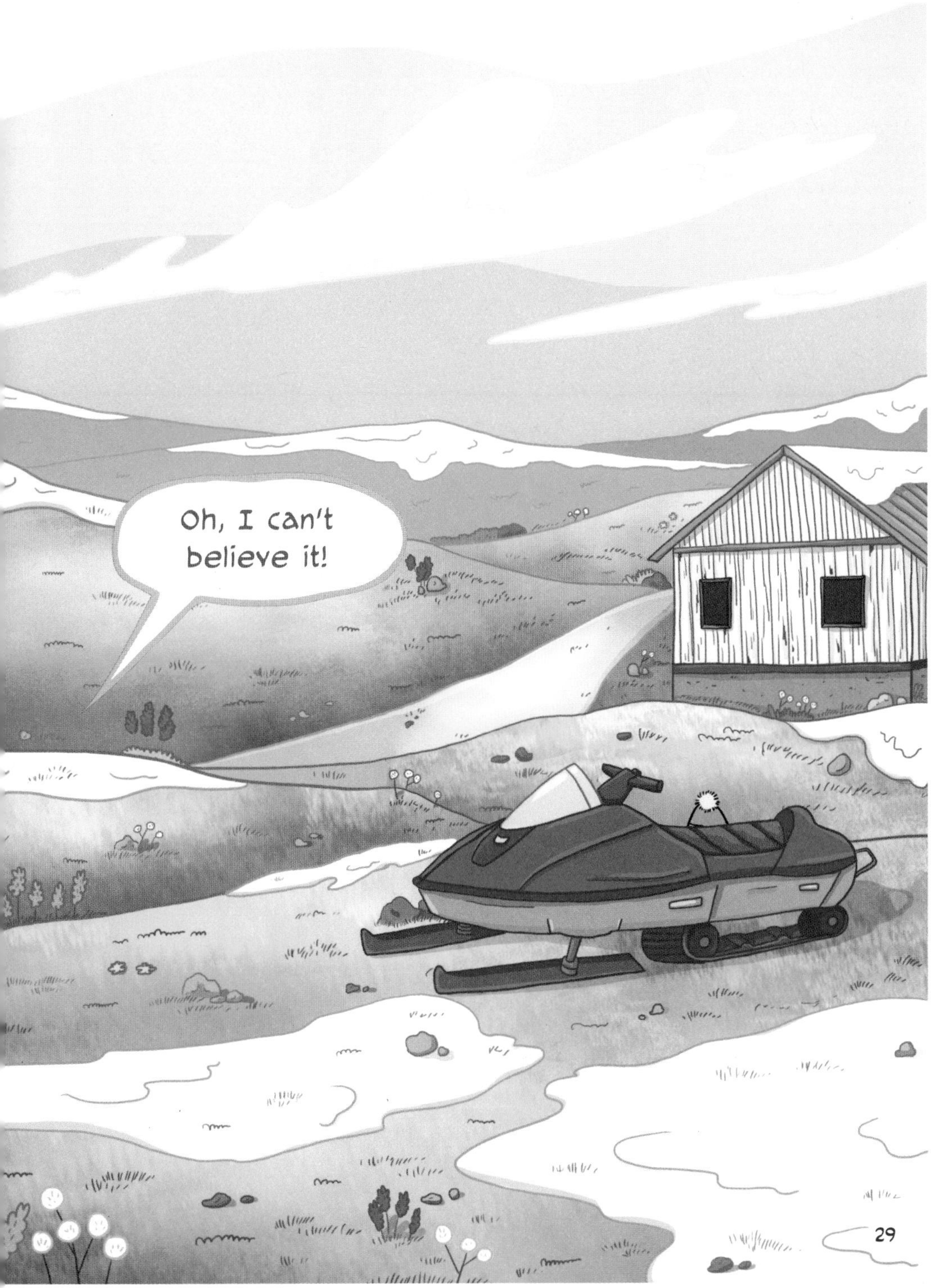
Oh, I can't believe it!

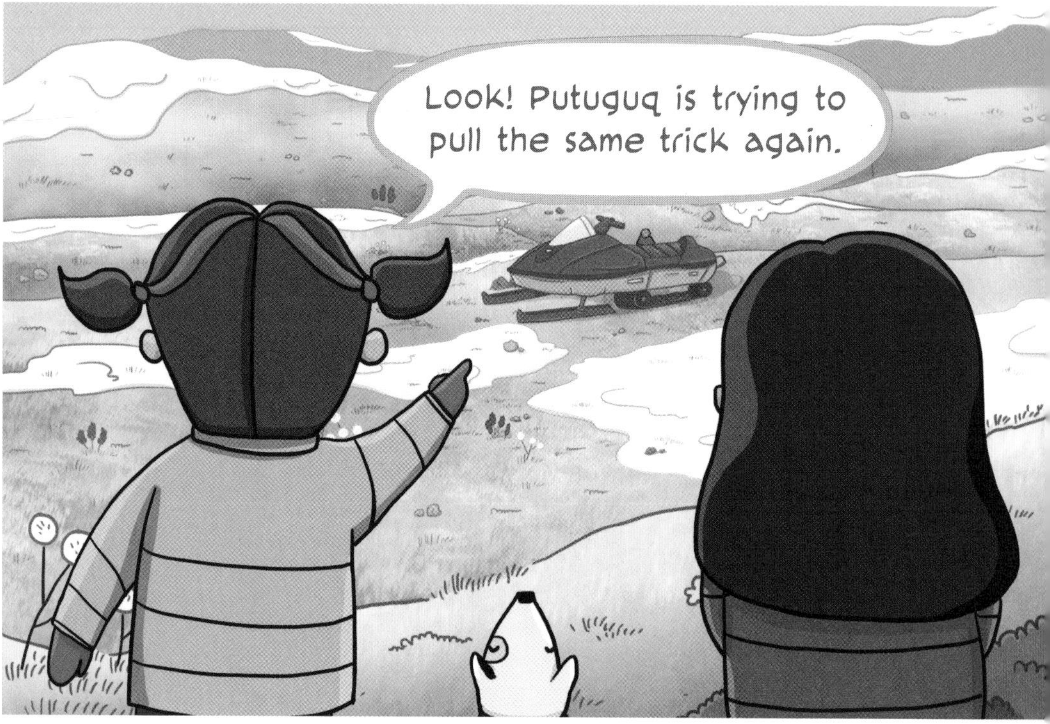
Look! Putuguq is trying to pull the same trick again.

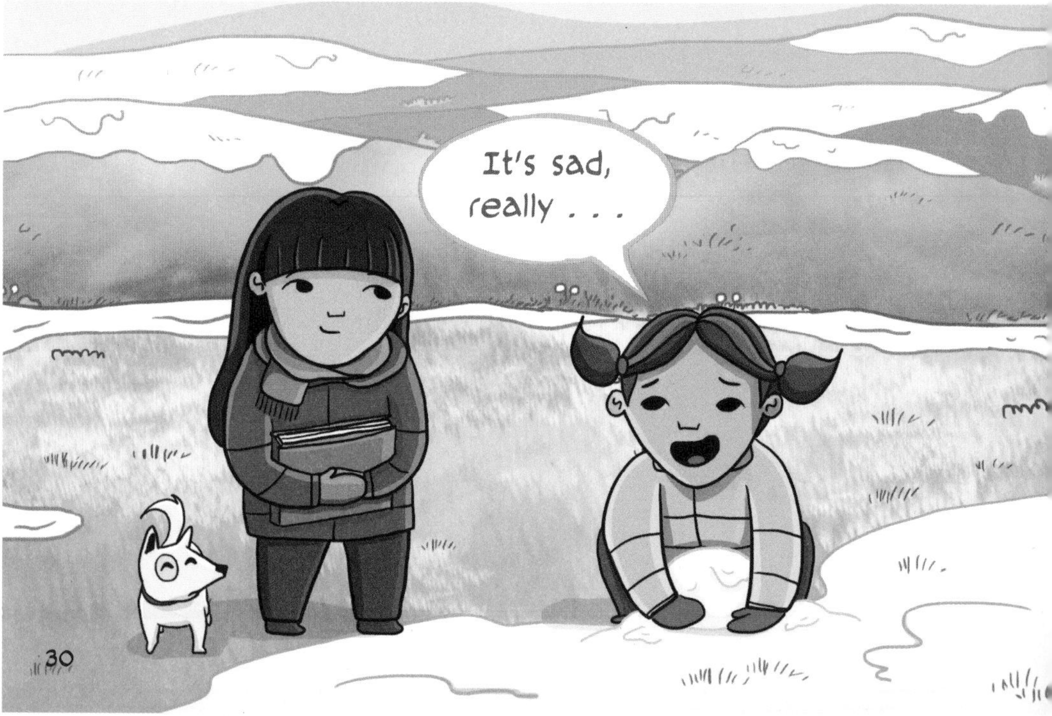
It's sad, really . . .

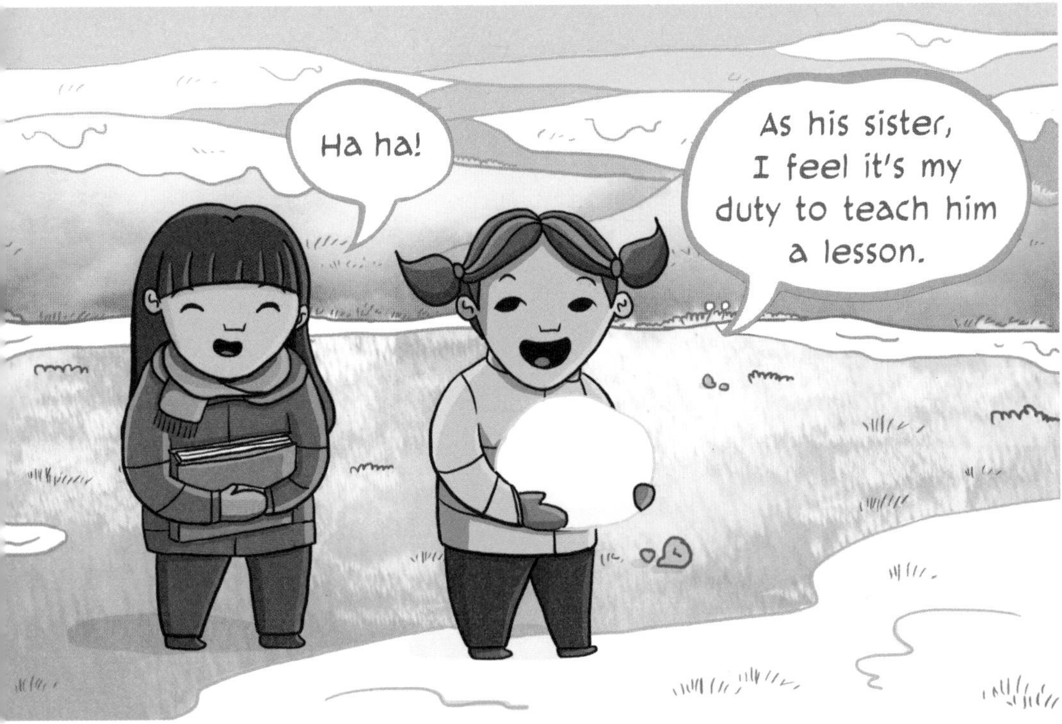
Ha ha!
As his sister, I feel it's my duty to teach him a lesson.

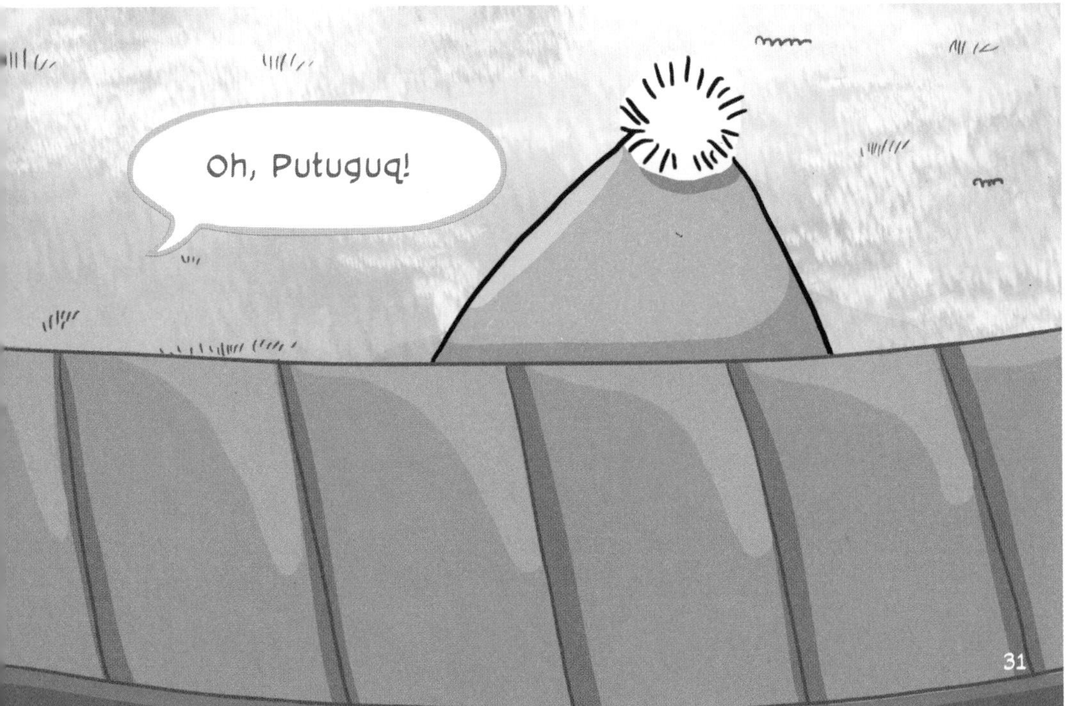
Oh, Putuguq!

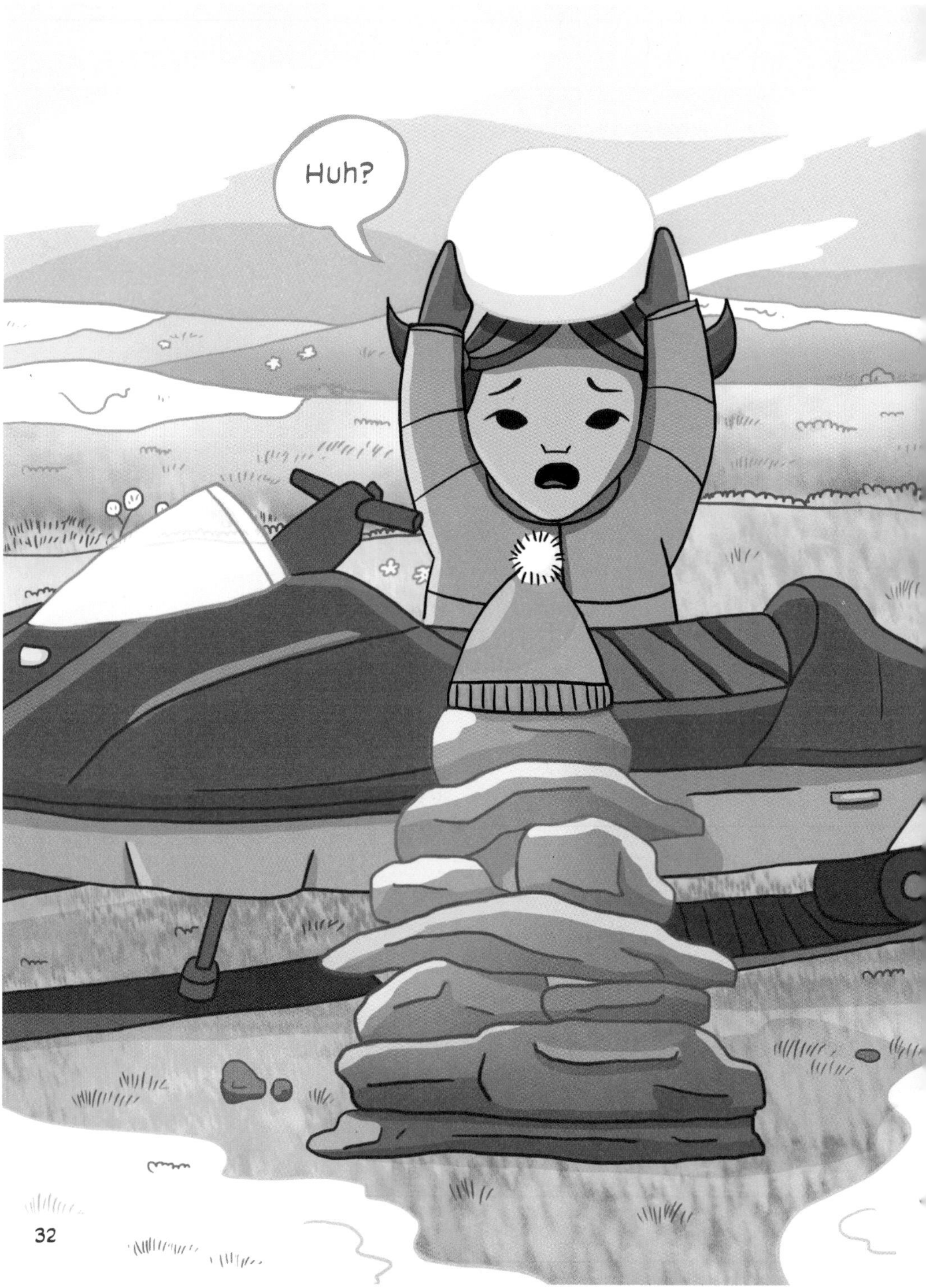
Huh?

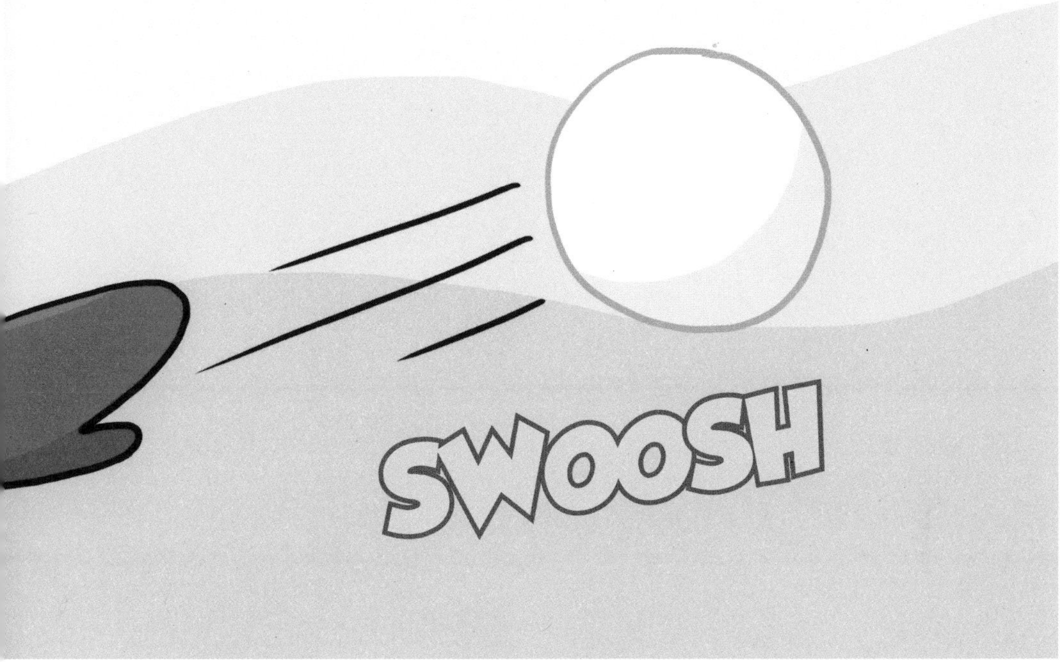
SWOOSH

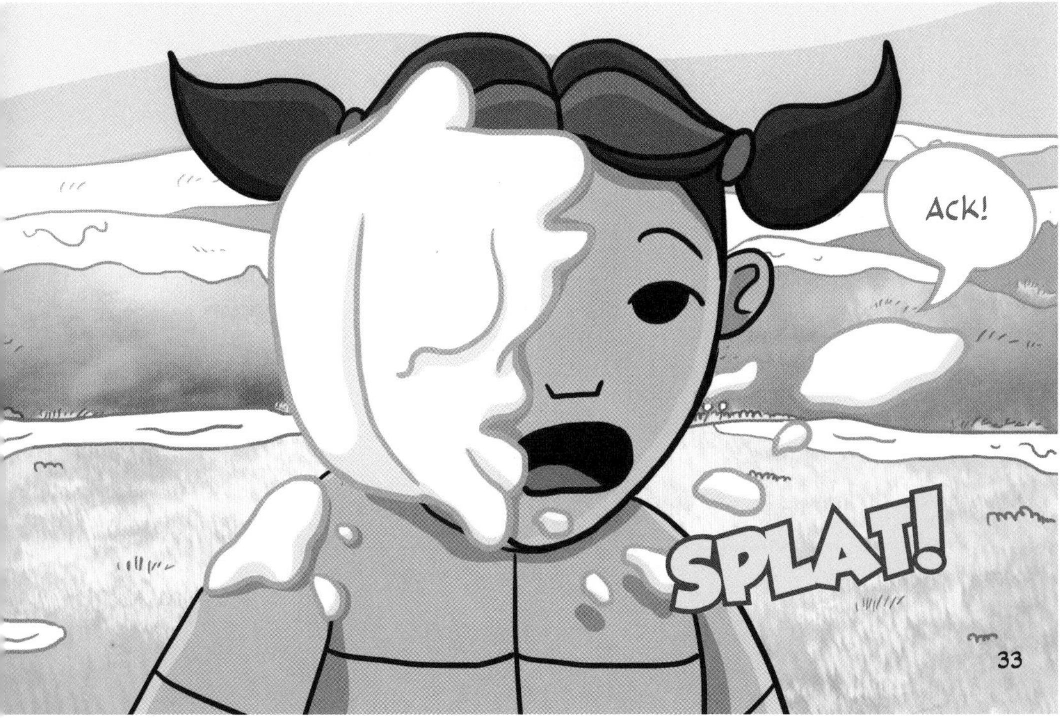
ACK!
SPLAT!

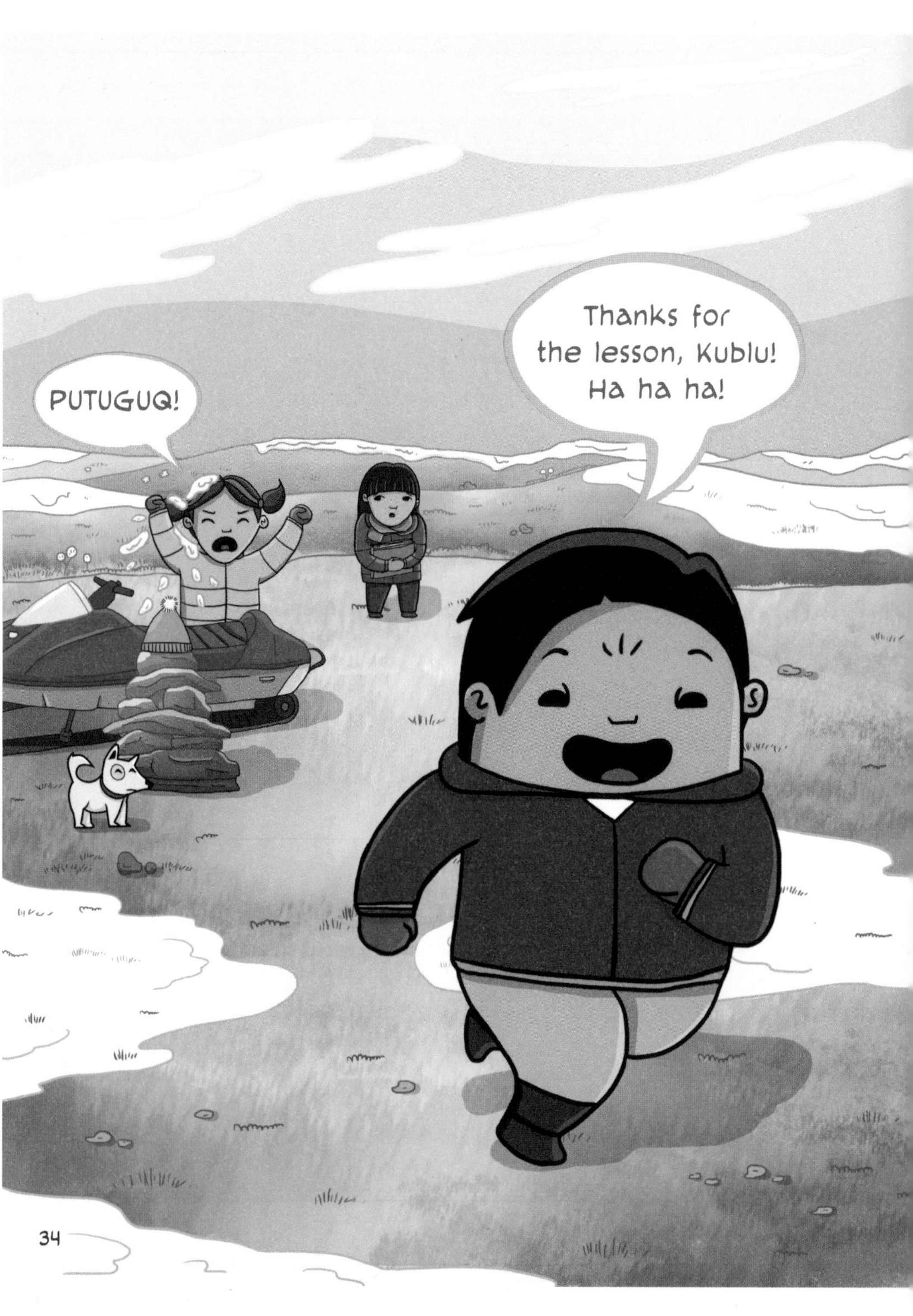
PUTUGUQ!
Thanks for the lesson, Kublu! Ha ha ha!

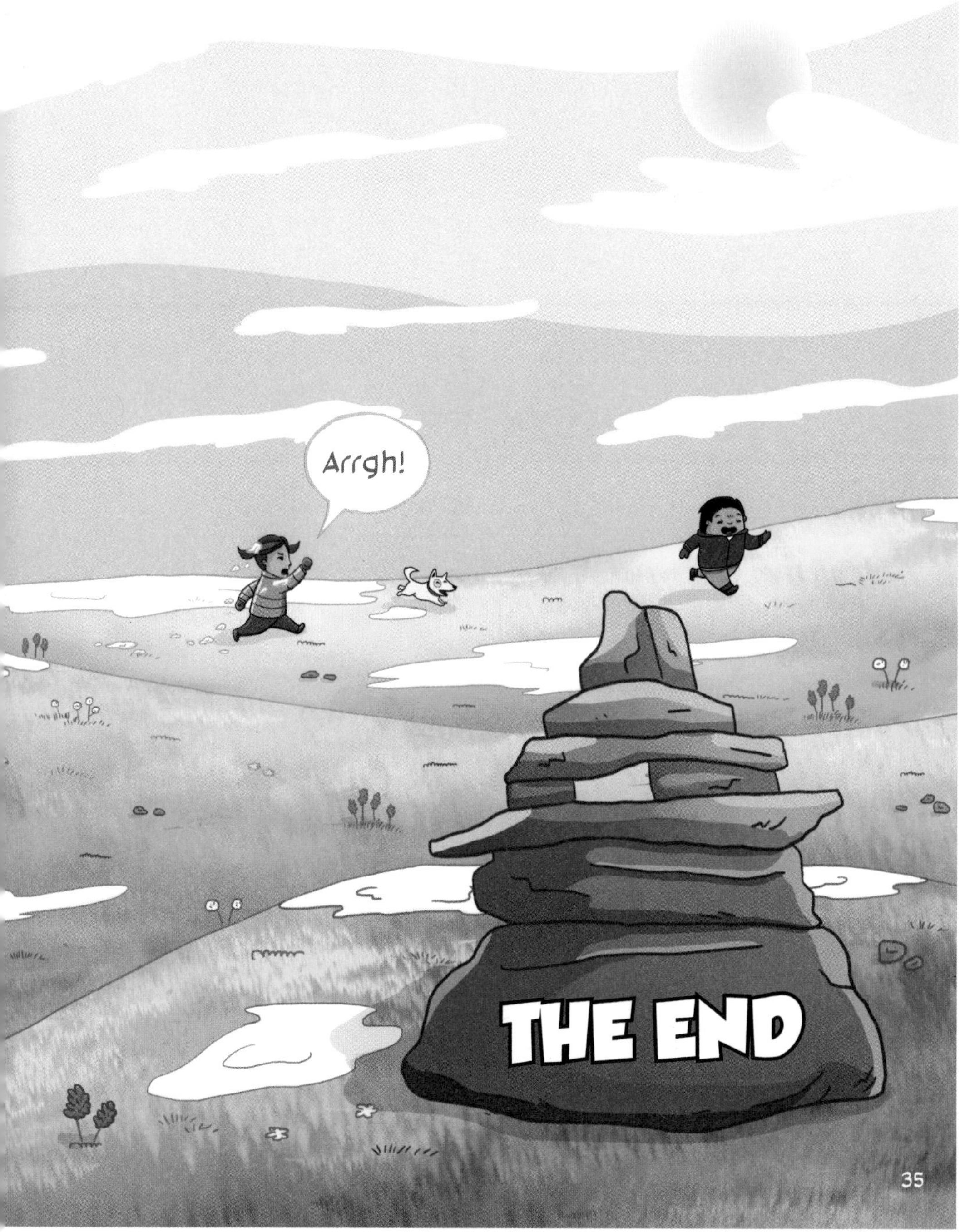
Arrgh!
THE END

INUKSUIT

singular INUKSUK

Inuksuit can be found all over the North American Arctic. These stone markers have been used as tools on the tundra for thousands of years by Inuit, as well as other cultures of the North. Inuksuit can be many different shapes and sizes, depending on their different purposes. 4,000-year-old inuksuit still stand in the Arctic. An inuksuk can be found on the flag of Nunavut.

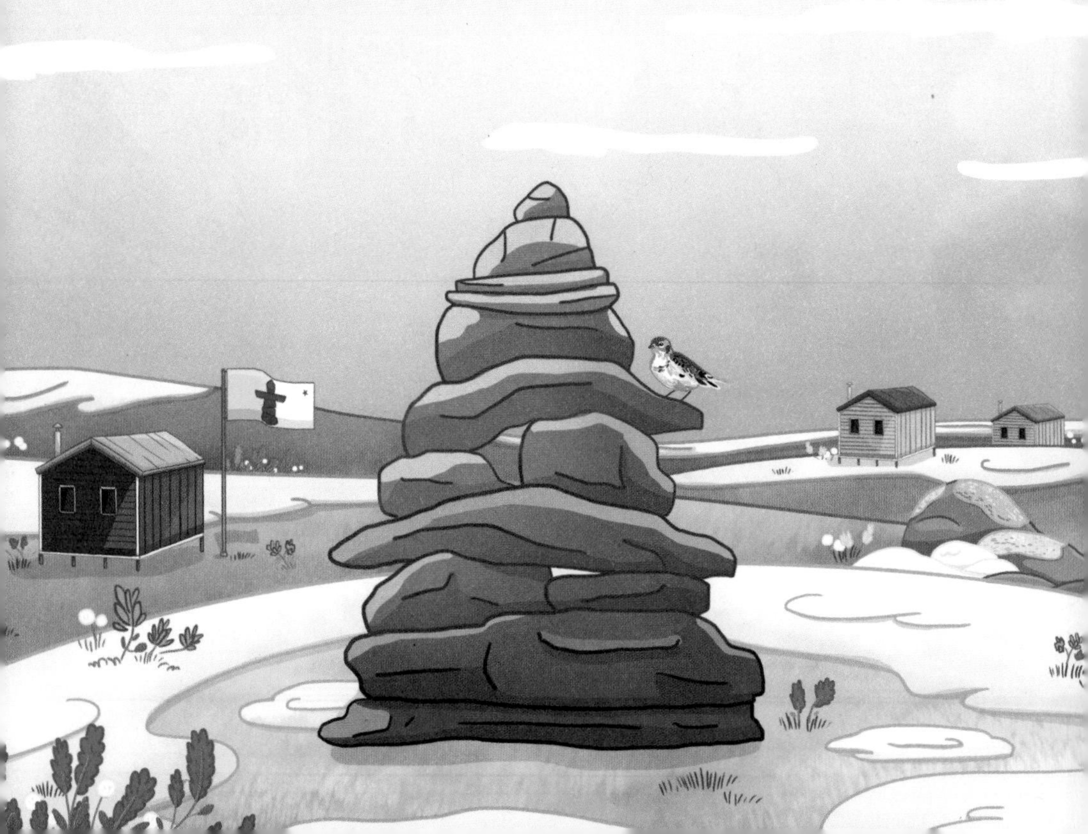

TUNIIT

singular TUNIQ

Tuniit, also called the Dorset people, inhabited the North American Arctic over 2,500 years ago, before the arrival of Inuit. Tuniit disappeared about 500 years ago. Old Inuit stories describe Tuniit as a shy yet immensely powerful people. They are sometimes described as giants. To find out more about the fascinating Tuniit, be sure to pick up *Tuniit: Mysterious Folk of the Arctic*, published by Inhabit Media.

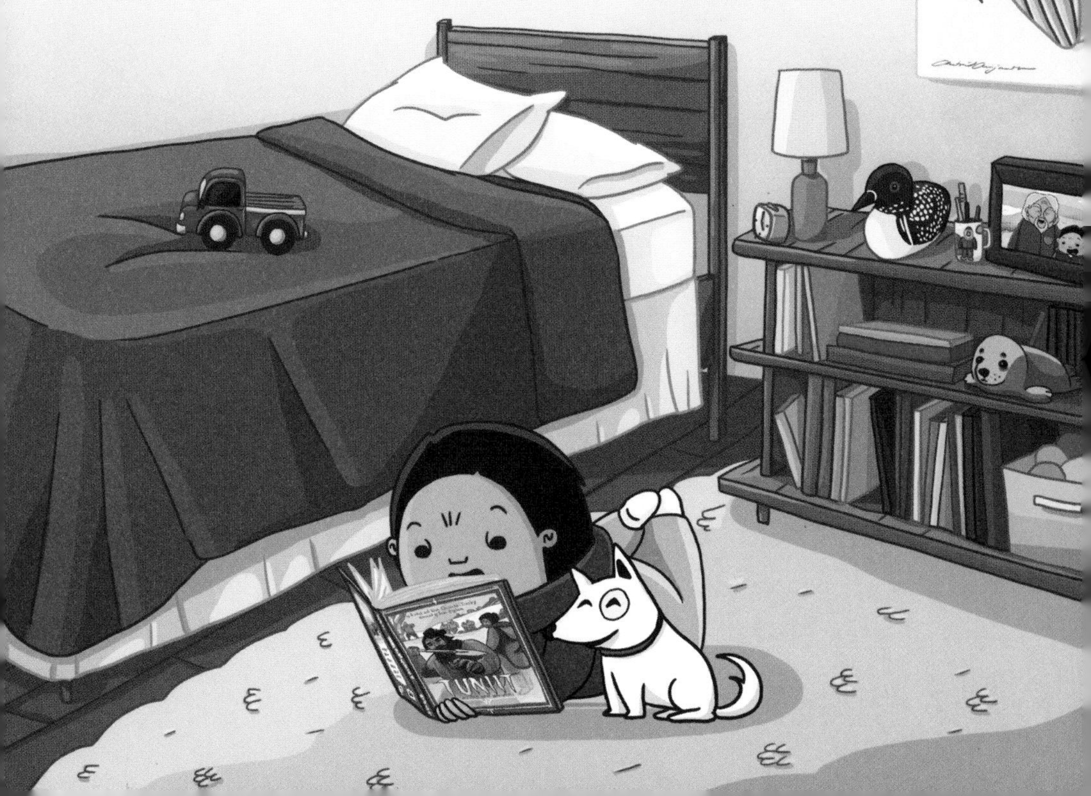

CONTRIBUTORS

Danny Christopher has travelled throughout the Canadian Arctic as an instructor for Nunavut Arctic College. He is the illustrator of *The Legend of the Fog*, *A Children's Guide to Arctic Birds*, and *Animals Illustrated: Polar Bear*. His work on *The Legend of the Fog* was nominated for the Amelia Frances Howard-Gibbon Illustration Award. He lives in Toronto with his wife, three children, and a puppy.

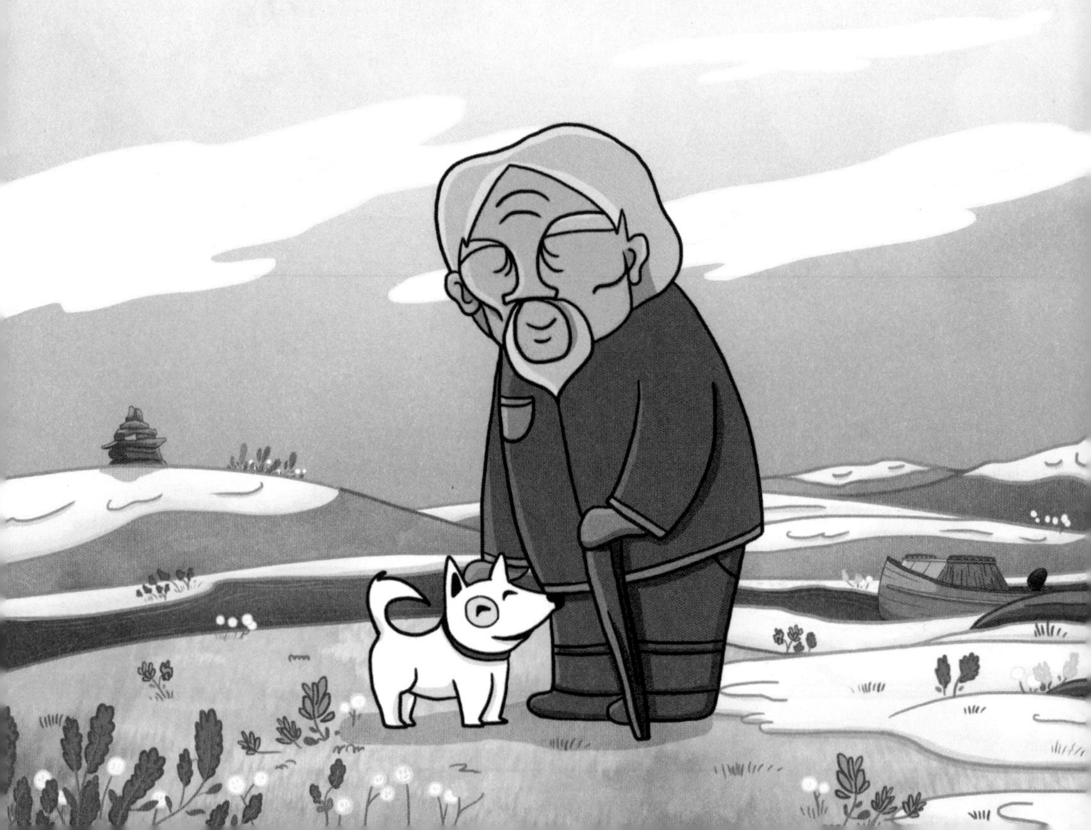

Astrid Arijanto is a designer and illustrator who spent her childhood drawing on any surface she could get her hands on: from papers to walls to all the white fences around her parents' house. Since then, her work has appeared in various media and publications across Canada and Asia. She lives in Toronto and spends most of her days designing and illustrating beautiful books. In her free time she enjoys travelling with her partner, exploring the great outdoors, and chasing after their wild and rambunctious puppy, Spanky.

INHABIT
MEDIA

Iqaluit • Toronto